COOL AS ICE

The #1 Sports Series for Kids

Matt Christopher®

COOL AS ICE

Text by Paul Mantell

LITTLE, BROWN AND COMPANY

New York ∾ Boston

To Chris and Beth

Little, Brown and Company

Hachette Book Group USA
237 Park Avenue , New York, NY 10017
Visit our Web site at www.lb-kids.com

www.mattchristopher.com

First Paperback Edition: April 2001

Matt Christopher® is a registered trademark
of Matt Christopher Royalties, Inc.

Text written by Paul Mantell

Library of Congress Cataloging-in-Publication Data

Mantell, Paul.
    Cool as ice : the #1 sports series for kids / Matt Christopher; text by Paul Mantell. — 1st ed.
        p.   cm.
    Summary: Two friends try to prove that size and race do not matter when playing hockey or any other sport.
    ISBN 978-0-316-13520-7 ISBN 0-316-13520-8
    [1. Hockey — Fiction.   2. Size — Fiction.   3. Race relations — Fiction.]   I. Matt Christopher.   II. Title.
PZ7.M31835 Co   2001
[Fic] — dc21   00-064754

PB: 10   9   8   7   6

COM-MO

Printed in the United States of America

COOL AS ICE

Chris Wells glided swiftly across the ice. In his head, he could hear the music he'd chosen for his newest routine — "Cool as Ice," by Flim-Flamma. Swaying to the hip-hop rhythm, he twisted his legs back and forth, picking up speed.

Faster and faster he went, streaking across the ice. Just when it looked like he was going to slam into the boards, he flung his weight hard to the right and went airborne!

Chris's body spun around twice before coming back down to the ice. His skates hit softly, and he lifted his arms in triumph.

Yes! he thought. *A perfect double lutz!*

He'd done the jump before, but had only perfected it a month ago. It was really hard, too. *Imagine how impossible a* triple *lutz must be,* he reflected. And yet, champion skaters did them all the time!

Chris went over to the boards to catch his breath. Looking around, he noticed a little boy on the other side of the rink, trying to learn how to skate backward. The kid's feet suddenly went out from under him, and he fell hard, right on his behind.

Chris smiled, but didn't laugh. He had been figure skating ever since the age of five. He remembered being just like that kid. He wouldn't have wanted anybody laughing at him.

Back then, it had been fun. Chris was able to do tricks and jumps other kids couldn't do without falling on their rear ends. But over the years, he had gotten tired of it all. Figure skating took up so much time! Working with his coach, practicing his routines . . . it wasn't a lot of fun, except for the occasional performance or competition. Even then, Chris sometimes got so tense that he didn't do his best — and *that* was no fun, either.

Oh, sure, he knew he was pretty good. Anyone watching him do his routines would have thought he was amazing for a kid his age. Unless, of course, they'd seen real champions compete. Chris knew he didn't measure up to that level, and was pretty sure he never would.

Worse, he wasn't sure he *cared* anymore. He was almost a teenager now, and was getting interested in other things. He wanted to hang out with kids — go to the mall, to movies, to football games — have fun!

He was twelve years old now, and he'd just about made up his mind to quit. The only problem was he didn't have the courage to break the news to his coach, or his mom.

Chris's mom was . . . well, she was *okay*, he guessed. He loved her, of course. It was just that she was kind of tough. Chris knew raising three kids by herself wasn't easy, so he didn't hold it against her.

His dad had left the family and moved out when Chris was nine, and his sisters, Hailey and Kyla, were six and four. The girls had just started taking figure skating lessons, but Mom said they could only afford lessons for one kid. Since Chris had already started and gotten pretty good, he got the lessons. At the time, he'd been happy about it. But that was back in the day when he still thought he could be an Olympic champion.

Chris shook his head disgustedly. What was he

doing here, spending his after-school hours working on a routine he was never even going to perform? What was the point?

There *was* no point. In fact, today was the day he put his foot down, he promised himself. He was going to quit. He was sick of figure skating. He needed something new in his life. But what?

Looking up at the big clock that hung over the center of the rink, he saw that it was nearly four o'clock. The hockey players would be here soon, to start their practice time. From four to seven, the rink was given over to hockey games and practices. Chris could hear them now, entering the rink and putting on their skates and padding. Lots of excited voices. He'd have to get off the ice to make room for them.

Well, he'd practiced enough for one day, anyway, Chris figured. It was always good to quit while you were ahead. As always, he felt a pang of envy as he watched the hockey players take over the rink, jostling each other, laughing and shouting. They were having fun. *He* wanted to have fun, too.

Stepping off the ice, Chris headed for his locker, where he proceeded to stow his skates and lace up his sneakers.

"Hey, Wells!"

Chris looked up. It was Teddy Chester, a kid Chris had been friends with back in first grade. They hadn't been close for the last couple years. Teddy was dressed in a black hockey uniform. He had his stick in his hand and was leaning on it, watching Chris.

"Hey, Teddy."

"Goin' out for hockey?" Teddy asked. He peered at the skates Chris had just put in the locker. "Oh, wait, I forgot. You're a *figure skater.*" He snorted. "Where's your spangled outfit?"

Chris scowled. Here it was again, more of the usual teasing. It was one of the worst parts of figure skating, all the razzing you took for supposedly being a sissy. People just didn't realize how tough you had to be, how strong — even if you were short and skinny like he was. "You know I don't wear stuff like that," he muttered.

"Figure skating is for wimps," Teddy said, shaking his head. "You a wimp, Wells?"

"Shut up, okay, Teddy?" Chris snapped back. "I'd like to see you try it."

"Shee-yuh!" Teddy laughed. "That'll be the day. Why don't you go out for hockey, man?"

Chris didn't feel like arguing with him. Nobody ever changed their minds when you argued with them. Besides, his mom would be waiting outside. "Later," he told Teddy, getting up and making for the exit.

As he passed the other boy, Chris felt himself being shoved lightly, just a subtle push. "Quit it," he told Teddy.

"Make me, wimp," Teddy shot back, dropping the stick and putting up his dukes.

Chris sighed deeply. "I'm not gonna fight with you, Teddy," he said. "You're way bigger than me. Pick on somebody your own size, huh?"

Teddy just laughed. Shaking his head, Chris kept going. Out in the front hallway, he could see the hockey players warming up out on the ice. It *did* look like fun.

He remembered how he had asked his mom if he could play, back when he was nine.

"It's way too dangerous," she said. "I don't want anything happening to that handsome face and those beautiful teeth. You'll thank me someday for keeping you away from that brutal nonsense."

Chris knew what she really had been afraid of. He was a short, skinny kid back then, and she didn't want him getting all his bones broken. Unfortunately, things hadn't improved much. He was twelve now, but he was only two inches taller and ten pounds heavier!

Chris scowled again. When was his growth spurt ever going to start? Half the kids in seventh grade were already thirteen, and many of them towered over him.

His old friend and next-door neighbor, Lynne St. James, was four inches taller than he was and twenty-five pounds of pure muscle heavier. She could beat him up anytime she wanted to, and both of them knew it. It was totally embarrassing. And the worst part was, Lynne was only eleven!

Chris went outside and got into the waiting car. His mom gave him a smile. "How'd practice go?" she asked.

"Okay," he mumbled.

They drove off toward home, through the leafy streets of Cedarville. The arena was in the wealthy part of town, not at all like the area where the Wellses lived. *You could fit two of our house into any of these,* Chris thought as he passed Teddy Chester's place.

Thinking about Teddy brought to mind his half-joking question about Chris trying out for hockey.

Well, why shouldn't I try out? he thought. *Maybe if I tell Mom I want to keep skating, but for a hockey team, she'll be all right with it. It's worth a try.*

"Hey, Mom?" he said, working up his courage.

"Mmm?"

He spit out the words before he chickened out. "Would you be very upset if I stopped taking skating lessons?"

Even though he was staring out of the car window, he could feel his mom turning her eyes toward him. "*What?*" she breathed.

"I mean, just for a while." Chris backed off immediately. "Kind of take a break from figure skating?"

There was a long silence as his mom considered this. "Chris, what's really going on?"

Chris shrugged. "I don't know. I guess I'm just tired of practicing the same moves, over and over again."

8

"But, honey, that's how you get better — you *know* that."

"I don't care!" Chris said, his frustration spilling out. "I'm tired of it! And besides, I'm never going to be a champion skater, so what's the point?"

Again, that long silence. "The point," his mom finally said, "is to learn to do something well. To put in the hard work and get the reward — the satisfaction of knowing you've done it."

Chris made a face, but said nothing.

"You know, if you stop skating, you'll gradually lose all the skills you've built up," she said.

Aha! Chris thought. She was softening just a little. Now was the time to press his advantage. "You're right," he acknowledged. "That's why I was thinking I wouldn't *stop* skating — not *exactly*."

"I'm not sure what you mean," she said.

"I mean, I'd like to play hockey this year instead."

His mom swung the car to the right and pulled over with a screeching of brakes. Putting the gear shift into park, she turned to look at him. "*Hockey!?*" she repeated, disbelieving. "You're joking, right?"

"Uh, no."

"What makes you think I'm going to allow you to play a brutal sport like hockey?"

"Because I asked you, and you want me to be happy?" he tried.

"Christopher, think," she said. "Use your head. You're what — five-three?"

"Five-four," he corrected her, squirming in his seat.

"You weigh what? Ninety pounds or something?"

Chris was silent. She'd nailed his weight right on the nose.

"Have you noticed the size of the kids who play in the Town League?" she asked. "Just take a look at them and ask yourself if you fit in."

"Well, what about hormone shots?" he said weakly.

She rolled her eyes. "Christopher, really. You're sure to start growing any time now. A year from now, maybe you'll be big enough. Why don't you keep figure skating till then, and —"

"I'm *through* with figure skating!" he yelled, astonishing himself and his mother with his pent-up frustration. "I want to try hockey! If you won't let me, I'm gonna hang up my skates altogether!"

"Honey," his mom pleaded, "be reasonable. Figure skating is beautiful, and civilized, and graceful. Hockey is rough, barbaric —"

"It's fun!"

"How would you know?"

"That's my point exactly!" he insisted. "If you won't let me try it, how am I going to find out if I like it?"

His mom sighed, worn out by the argument. "Look," she said. "It's not just that you might get injured. Hockey equipment is expensive, and I'm already working two jobs to support this family. Your dad's no help at all, goodness knows . . ."

"How 'bout if I call Dad and ask him to buy me the equipment?" Chris suggested. It was a dangerous suggestion, and he knew it. Nothing made his mom angrier than talking about the man who'd walked out on her.

"Sure, go ahead, call him!" she said. He could hear the anger in her voice, making it sound artificially high and choked up. "Then he can be the good guy, and I'll be the evil, mean mom. Why not?"

He could see the tears falling from her eyes and decided it was time to back off. He knew his mom worked really hard to support them all, and that his dad was always late with the child support payments. He felt sorry now that he'd brought up the subject.

They rode home in silence, each thinking their private thoughts. It occurred to Chris that getting up at six in the morning to take him to weekend games wouldn't be a problem for his mom. She got up that early anyway, to go to her weekend job at the laundromat. But he decided to save that argument for another time. He'd caused her enough pain for one day.

2

ad? It's me . . . Chris."

"Boomer!" His father's voice exploded on the other end of the line, even though Chris had spoken in a whisper, so as not to wake his mom. "Boomer, it's great to hear from you!"

Chris winced. His dad had always called him that, from the time he was two or three. At that age, Chris had been kind of chubby, and his dad always liked to fantasize about what a big, tall bruiser his son was going to be.

Well, that was then; this was now. Chris hadn't grown tall and broad-shouldered. He'd grown up to be a whole different kind of kid. And Chris's dad had missed the whole thing.

Chris didn't call him very much. That way, he could tell how often his dad missed him enough to pick up a phone. It worked out to every two months or so. As for live visits, they happened about once a year, usually around Chris's birthday.

His dad traveled a lot for work; always had. That was probably what led to the divorce, Chris figured. Even before then, his dad hadn't been around much.

"So, you finally decided to call the old man for a change!" his dad continued, cheerfully guilt-tripping Chris. "What's the occasion?"

"No occasion, Dad," Chris said softly. "I just wanted to talk to you about something important."

"Oh! Well, sure, Boomer. Fire away! What's on your mind?"

His dad was a salesman, and talked like one. Always full of enthusiasm and good humor. Well, sometimes — like now — Chris didn't feel like matching his dad's mood. Chris wasn't buying anything at the moment. In fact, he was *selling* something.

"Dad . . ." He hated bringing his dad into the argument between him and his mom. It was kind of underhanded, actually. But Chris was desperate. For three days, his mom had been saying no to him trying out for hockey.

14

He'd run out of arguments, and he was running out of time. Tryouts for Town League ended the day after tomorrow! If he didn't convince her by then, it would be too late!

"Dad, I was thinking of trying out for hockey. . . ."

"Hockey? Great!" his dad exclaimed. "Fantastic!"

"Well, Mom won't let me." There it was. He'd just dropped the bomb.

"What!?" His dad's tone turned angry. "Why won't she?"

"She says it's too rough, and that I'll get hurt. She wants me to keep figure skating."

"What? Are you still doing that?" It pained Chris to be reminded that his dad didn't even know *that*. He had no clue at all about what was going on in Chris's life.

"I told her I wanted to quit," Chris said.

"Good for you!"

"Dad, it's not that — I *like* figure skating."

"Yeah, yeah, of course you do. I didn't mean to imply —"

"But I'm tired of it," Chris went on. "I wanna have some fun, skate with other kids. But Mom thinks I'm too small and lightweight."

15

"Put her on the phone. I'll talk to her."

"Dad, she's sleeping. It's ten o'clock, and she gets up at five in the morning to go to work."

"Gee, does she really?" His dad seemed shocked.

"And she also says she can't afford to buy me hockey equipment," Chris added, pressing the point.

"I . . . I've been meaning to catch up on the checks, Boomer," his dad said, sounding apologetic. "Listen, I'll buy you the equipment. And I'm gonna be better about the checks. Business was bad there for a while, but things are turning around now."

"Sure, Dad," Chris said, sighing.

"Now wake your mom up and put her on the phone."

Chris hated to do it, but what choice did he have? He crossed the hall, went into her room, and gently shook her awake. "Dad's on the phone," he told her.

His mom shot up in bed. "What does he want this time?" she said, already angry. She threw off the covers and picked up the extension next to her bed. "Hello?"

Chris backed out of the room slowly, leaving the rest of the "discussion" to his parents. He didn't want to be in the middle of the fireworks. When his mom and his dad started arguing, it was a war zone. And he had no doubt they were going to argue over this.

He had just about reached the safety of his bed when he heard the yelling start. "*Hockey!?* Christopher! Get in here!"

He didn't move. If she wanted him that much, she'd have to come and get him. Luckily, it never came to that. The argument went on, his mom forgetting about him as she screamed at his dad over the phone. Chris covered his head with the blanket and tried not to listen.

Then he heard the phone slam down and his mom sobbing in the next room. Chris was sorry now that he'd called his dad. His poor mom had it so rough as it was, and now he had to go and drag Dad back into her life, opening all the old wounds.

Chris was sorry he'd even asked to play hockey. He should be making her life easier, not harder, he scolded himself. Reluctantly, he decided that if she didn't let him play hockey, he would stick with figure skating, just to make her happy.

The next morning, Chris woke up at eight. His mom had already gone to the local laundromat where she worked on Saturdays — one of her two jobs, not counting raising Chris and his sisters.

Chris felt worse than ever about bothering her. It made him see himself as a bad kid, and he hated the feeling. He decided to go next door and see Lynne St. James. Hanging around with her always seemed to cheer him up.

He and Lynne had been inseparable ever since her family had moved to Mercer Street, back when he was five and she was four. She remembered his dad — and he remembered hers, who had died five years ago.

They walked to school together pretty much every morning, and they took a lot of heat for it. Kissing sounds sometimes followed them down the street as they neared the school entrance. "Chris has a girl-friend!" the guys would tease Chris in the locker room. "Lynne's got a boyfriend," Lynne would hear in line in the school cafeteria. "It's Miss Big and Mister Little!" somebody had once commented.

Lynne could have beat any of those kids up, if she'd wanted to, Chris thought with a smile. She was kind of pretty, with her wavy blond hair and blue eyes — but she was also bigger and stronger and way more athletic than most of the boys. Still, she never got violent with anybody. Lynne was a gentle person. And Chris didn't care what people said behind their backs. Guys and girls *could* be best friends, and he and Lynne were living proof.

He got dressed. Then he wolfed down a couple donuts and a glass of milk — food designed to fatten him up, though it never did — and went next door.

Lynne was out back, feeding the family's pet chicken. "Hey!" he called to her as he swung open the backyard gate.

"Hey, yourself!" she shouted back, still busy with her morning routine. The chicken cooed lovingly as Lynne changed its water and took a big brown egg from the coop. "Thanks, Buc-Buc," she told the bird, then turned to face Chris. "Wuzzup?"

"Nothin'," he said, sighing miserably. "Busy?"

"Just the usual. Come on, you look terrible. What's going on?"

"It's a long story."

"I've got a long list of pets to feed. Walk with me, and let's hear it." She led him into the house, where she fed the rabbit, then the finches, then the fish, and the hamster, and the dog, and the cat.

19

Lynne's house might as well have been a zoo, Chris reflected as he told her what had happened. He loved animals, too. He would have had a pet if his mom hadn't been allergic to everything under the sun, from fur to feathers. But Lynne absolutely was bezonkers about them. She wanted to be a vet someday.

As far as Chris was concerned, she already *was* one. Her animals were never sick, they all got along, and they seemed perfectly happy. Right now, he wished he was one of them.

"Wow," she said as he finished his tale of woe. "So what are you gonna do now?"

"I don't know," he said.

"Are you gonna try out anyway?"

"Should I?"

Lynne shrugged and waggled her eyebrows. "I don't see why not. If you got on the team, it would prove to your mom you're good enough. And if she still says no, you can always back out of it."

"Yeah!" As usual, Lynne was full of good ideas.

"One thing, though," she interrupted. "We're gonna have to get you ready."

"What do you mean?"

"Toughen you up."

"You don't think I'm tough enough?"

"Chris," she said, giving him a look. "It's true, there's not supposed to be any checking in Town League hockey. But you know there's lots of contact, plenty of hits when guys take off after the puck. And fights happen once in a while, too. You've got to learn how to stand up to the punishment."

"Oh." He wasn't sure he understood. "Like how?"

"Come with me." She led him downstairs to her basement rec room and fished two sets of boxing gloves out of a carton. "Here," she said, handing him a pair. "Put these on, and let's see what you're made of."

"Huh? I'm not gonna box with you!"

"Why? Because I'm a girl and you think I can't take it?" she challenged him.

"No! I think the exact opposite, actually." Chris put the gloves on. "Okay, let's spar a little." She put up her dukes, and so did he. They began circling each other, throwing little punches. Then, out of nowhere, Lynne threw a right hand at him. Before he could get his gloves up to block the blow, it hit him square on the side of his head.

Chris's legs wobbled, and he dropped like a rock.

21

The next thing he knew, he was staring up into Lynne's worried face. Her big blue eyes were looking down at him through strands of wavy blond hair. "Are you okay?" she asked.

"What are those flies circling around your head?" he asked her.

"Oh, boy," she said. "You're seeing stars."

"No," Chris insisted dopily. "They're flies . . . I think . . ."

"Whoo," Lynne said, shaking her head and blowing out a deep breath. "When did you say tryouts were?"

"Tomorrow night."

"Well . . . we've sure got our work cut out for us."

"Chris?" His mom's voice, ragged but soft, sounded on the other side of his bedroom door. "Honey, can we talk for a minute?" Chris glanced at his alarm clock. Two P.M. She must have just gotten back from work.

"Come on in." Chris put down his history textbook and swung around in his swivel chair as his mom came into the room. "I'm sorry, Mom," he said right off. "I shouldn't have called Dad last night. That was mean —"

"No, honey, that's okay," she said. "I guess I didn't realize how strongly you felt about this hockey stuff."

"It's okay," Chris said.

"No, look. I made a few phone calls to some parents of kids who play hockey — Emily Stoddard, Erna Nagel, Emily Canelo — and they all say I

23

ought to let you try out. Apparently, there's no hitting allowed —"

"No checking," Chris corrected her.

"Whatever, they assured me it's reasonably safe, and well supervised. And your dad says he'll pay for the equipment, so I guess you can give it a try."

"Mom! You mean it?"

She sniffed. "If you've got your heart set on playing hockey, and it means that much to you, then I won't stand in your way. Just promise me you'll be careful, okay? I don't want my sweet baby to get hurt." Her chin quivered and big tears welled in her eyes.

Chris hugged her tightly. "Thanks, Mom," he whispered, on the verge of tears himself. "You're the best."

"Just a few conditions —" His mom gently freed herself from his grasp.

Uh-oh, thought Chris. *Here it comes.*

"You've got to promise me you'll stay away from any fighting or physical contact."

"Mom, it's hockey!" Chris protested. "Guys knock into each other. Sometimes they get mad and stuff happens."

"At least promise you'll do your best to stay out of it."

"Okay, okay, I promise."

"And once the season's over, you'll go back to your figure skating lessons."

"Mom!"

"Christopher . . ."

He sighed loudly. "Okay, I promise," he said.

"You've put in way too much effort to just throw it all away on a whim," she pronounced.

Chris said nothing. It was a big concession, considering he'd told her he was giving it up. But he was getting a big concession in return. Fair was fair. At least now he could try out knowing that if he made the team, he could go ahead and play. And that was worth a lot!

Saturday afternoons and evenings were "free-skate" times at the rink, and the place was crowded with a mixed group of skaters. There were parents teaching their children, holding on to their arms as the kids slipped and staggered across the ice, or held on to the boards for dear life.

There were couples skating hand in hand, and a few stray figure skaters struggling to find some room to practice their moves. There were also a couple of wise-guy kids Chris knew — Lance Farrier and Chuckie McHugh — ducking in and out among the other skaters, trying to surprise them and throw them off balance. Whenever they made someone slip and fall, they laughed and slapped each other five.

Jerks, Chris thought as he stepped out onto the ice. He hated people who laughed at other people's misfortunes.

He and Lynne had arranged to meet here at six. They'd figured most of the kids and families would have gone home to supper by then, and date night wouldn't really have gotten started (at eight, the rink went into "light-show mode," with strobes and disco lights turning the place into a romantic wonderland).

But here it was, six o'clock, and the rink was mobbed with people. He craned his neck, trying to find Lynne among them. No such luck.

By six-thirty, the crowd was finally beginning to thin out — and that was when Lynne finally showed up. "Where've you been?" he asked. "I rung your bell on the way here, figuring we could give you a lift, but you weren't home."

"I was out digging up some equipment," she said. "I borrowed a stick, a helmet, and some padding for you to use at tryouts tomorrow. Figured you'd need it."

"Oh. Yeah," Chris said, realizing for the first time how totally unprepared he was.

"I think it'll fit," Lynne told him. "I got it off Bobby Cosmillo's little brother."

"Gee, thanks," Chris said with a smirk. Bobby Cosmillo's brother Nick was ten years old.

"You want to try the stuff on now? It's in my locker."

"Later," Chris told her. "I've been waiting for half an hour, and we can't use sticks anyway, since it's not hockey time. Let's just practice."

She led him out to the far end of the rink. "Okay," she said. "Let's say the puck's been sent down-ice, and we're both trailing it. I'll give you a head start. You've got to reach it and send it back out of your end before I get to you."

"Where's the puck?" he asked.

Lynne frowned, then reached into her pocket and pulled out a piece of paper. Crumpling it up into a ball, she said, "Here's the puck." With that, she tossed it into the corner. "Go!" she shouted, and Chris took off after it.

He got to the "puck" and kicked at it with his skate, sending it to his left. But before he could get out of her way, Lynne slammed him into the boards from behind. "Ooof!" Chris grunted, wincing in pain.

"You've gotta get out of there quicker, or you're gonna get creamed," she told him.

"Gonna? I just *did* get creamed!"

"Hey, don't complain. I took it easy on you," she said.

"You sure you've never played hockey?" he asked her, flexing his sore back.

"Well, there was that summer I played roller hockey," she said. "Let's just say I know how to hit."

"I'll say."

"You wanna take a hit at me?" she asked.

"Sure, why not?"

So they set the play up again, only this time Lynne went in after the puck first. Chris leaped into the air, determined to put a hard hit on her, girl or no girl. But Lynne, knowing he was coming, got out of the way faster than he could ever have imagined. Chris slammed into the boards where she had been a second earlier. "Oww!" he yelled, his funny bone on fire.

"Gotta anticipate," she told him, smiling.

"I anticipate winding up in the hospital if we keep on practicing like this!" he said, only half joking.

Half an hour later, Chris called an early halt to their practice. He figured he'd be banged up enough tomorrow as it was. He didn't want to be too sore to try out!

His backside hurt especially. Lynne had decked him on it several times with hard hits. She was unbelievably strong — or else, she was just so much heavier than he was that when he hit her, he bounced backward onto his rear end.

"You belong in the NHL," he told her as they skated off the ice and headed for the locker room.

"Yeah, shee-yuh!" she laughed, slapping him on the back so hard that he winced in pain.

At least he'd learned how to anticipate and avoid

direct hits from other players. He knew that would be important if he ever made it into the Town League.

"Thanks for helping me out," he told Lynne as he tried on the equipment she'd borrowed for him. "Yeah, this stuff fits about right."

"Great. You're gonna be fine, Chris. Don't worry."

"Yeah, right, 'Don't worry.' I've never played hockey in my life. Like I'm really gonna step out there and be an instant sensation!"

"You never know," Lynne told him with a smile. "You might surprise yourself. Remember, Town League isn't exactly a bunch of all-stars. You might get three or four really good players on a team — and that team would be in first place. It's not like Traveling Team or anything."

Chris felt relieved by her words, but just a little. Truth was, he'd been having second thoughts about this whole plan of his, ever since his mom gave her permission. When he'd had to fight against her opposition, he'd thought only of the fun he could have. But once she'd agreed to let him play, all his doubts — about his size, his toughness, the teasing he would take when he showed up at tryouts — began to close in on him.

He knew there was no checking allowed in Town League. He also knew those rules were routinely ignored. He'd been at games once or twice, and had even seen one kid get a concussion when another player's stick hit him just below the helmet.

He wondered if the other kids would hit him especially hard. Bullies always picked on the littlest kids, he knew. And what if they found out about his figure skating? That would be sure to make him a target.

His butt was sore already. What would it feel like when he'd been decked by the likes of Teddy Chester?

Stepping onto the ice at Town League hockey try-outs was, for Chris, like walking into a familiar place that had suddenly become a hall of funny mirrors. Everything was familiar, but totally twisted and changed. Everything the same, yet different.

Instead of the usual, graceful skaters, all around him were kids in uniform, carrying sticks, practicing sudden stops or quick turns. At figure skating time, skaters ignored each other, each in his or her own little world, gliding to whatever music the audio guy was playing that day.

Now, kids were shouting across the rink, bumping each other, and laughing. Pairs of boys passed the puck back and forth with their sticks. The result was so much noise that if any music had been playing, it surely would have been drowned out.

Even the shapes of the skaters were different. Figure skaters looked like people. But these kids — Chris included — looked more like astronauts with sticks!

Every kid had a helmet, shoulder and elbow pads, knee pads and shin guards, not to mention padded gloves. All of this equipment meant it was a lot harder to skate gracefully — and most of them didn't. It was more a "swing your arms out like a monkey and push forward" thing, Chris thought with a smile.

The smile quickly faded, though. In fact, Chris was so nervous, he could barely breathe. So he nearly jumped out of his skin when a coach's whistle blew not far from his ear.

There was a ripple of laughter, and Chris saw a pair of kids snickering at him. They must have noticed the way he'd reacted.

One of them lifted his helmet off his head, and Chris saw that it was Teddy Chester. "Hey, Peanut," he greeted Chris, clapping him on the back. "Your mom decided to let you play with the big boys, huh?"

"Zip it, Chester," Chris shot back. He might have been little, but he was tough — tougher than any of them realized. So what if Lynne had knocked him out with one punch yesterday? He'd gotten up again, hadn't he?

Chris skated away from Teddy and his pal and circled around once before coming to a stop facing the coach, a big, grizzled man with bushy eyebrows and a hard stare.

"Okay, you boys," he shouted so that everyone could hear him. "Listen up! I'm Coach Flanagan, for those of you I don't already know. Many of you have played Town League hockey before, so this tryout is just for us to see how much bigger and better you've gotten in the off-season."

There was laughter from some boys in the crowd, and excited nods and cheers. Looking around, Chris saw that some of the boys towered over him. Even those that were his height were much stockier, like tightly packed barrels of cement.

He saw three kids whispering together and pointing at him — no, wait a minute, they were pointing *past* him.

Chris looked over his shoulder and saw who they were pointing at. In back of the crowd of circling kids was one boy who towered over all the rest. He had to be six feet two at least. And big, too; strong and muscular, with a scowl on his face that was almost scary. Not only that — he was the only African American there.

Chris wondered if that was why the boys were pointing at him, or if it was only because they were impressed with his size and build. He made a mental note to introduce himself to the kid later, just to be friendly.

"We've got twelve- and thirteen-year-olds here together tonight," Coach Flanagan was saying. *Aha,* Chris said to himself. *No wonder some of the kids are so big.*

"During the season, twelves and thirteens play in separate leagues. But tonight's tryout is also for the Traveling Team, and Coach Berman is here looking for talent. The traveling squad is made up of twelves and thirteens combined, so that's why we've combined the tryouts."

Chris looked over at Coach Berman, then at Teddy Chester. He knew Teddy would get picked for Cedarville's traveling team, the Screaming Eagles. He'd been on the team last year and never stopped talking about it. Chris wondered if the new kid in the back, the big one, would make it — he sure looked like an athlete.

"We're gonna start with some skating drills," Coach Flanagan said. "Speed and agility. You can see how Coach Berman is laying out the cones. We'll time you as you navigate them, then skate straight back our way. Okay? Line up!"

Chris got in line, content to be near the back. He wanted to watch the other kids try it first, so he could see what they were doing right or wrong. The first thing he noticed was how careful most of the boys were being, like they were afraid to mess up. That made them tense, so that they sometimes caught an edge and tripped, even fell on their faces.

Funny, Chris thought. *The more careful they are, the clumsier they get.* He told himself to stay loose and not worry about falling. This course looked pretty easy. No reason not to take it in a hurry.

"Name?" Coach Flanagan asked Chris when it was his turn.

"Chris Wells."

"Wells. Okay, little guy, show us what you can do. Ready. Set. Go!" He clicked his stopwatch.

Chris took off, running at first to work up speed.

Then, with just a slight twist of his hips and knees, he zigzagged back and forth between the cones. He took the curve at the corner of the rink, then headed back at full speed. As he passed Coach Flanagan, he saw him raise the stopwatch and click it.

As Chris skidded to a quick stop, he heard the murmur rise from the group of assembled kids. They were talking about him! He realized with a rush of excitement that his run had impressed them.

"Wow!" Coach Flanagan said, staring at his stopwatch. "This kid can skate! Where'd you come from, Wells?"

Chris grinned, knowing the coach didn't really expect an answer.

"Nice job!" Coach Flanagan told him with a grin and a nod. "Next!"

Chris skated over to the boards to watch the last few kids go through the drill. One of them was the black kid, who took the course amazingly quickly for his size, though not nearly as fast as Chris had done.

"Okay, now we'll try it in reverse," Coach Flanagan announced, and the line formed again for the next drill.

Chris saw the black kid standing by himself and

decided this was the moment to introduce himself. He skated over and said, "Hi, I'm Chris."

The kid turned slowly and looked at him, the scowl never leaving his face. "So?" he asked.

"So, nothing. It's just my name, that's all."

"Okay. You can go now." The kid never took his eyes off him.

Chris didn't know what to do. He'd never been treated quite this rudely, right to his face. "Um . . . what's your name?" he finally got the nerve up to ask.

"Derek Morgan," the boy said.

"Well, hi," Chris said, trying a smile. He stood there, waiting for Derek to say something back. Anything.

Finally, he did. "What, do you want me to shake your hand or something?" Derek cocked his head, indicating the discussion was over.

"Nice to meet you," Chris said, then skated away. "*Not,*" he muttered under his breath. Boy, what an attitude! As if Chris had offended him just by being friendly! Chris shook his head in disbelief, but he couldn't deny that he felt hurt. What had he done to deserve being treated like that?

Chris waited till everyone else had gone, then

took his turn at the backward-skating drill. By then, he'd gotten over being shaken up, and he performed the drill almost as well as he'd done it forward. Again, there was that ripple of impressed murmuring, and Chris saw Coach Flanagan shaking his head and smiling as he wrote down Chris's time.

After a few more drills, all of which Chris aced, the players were given a five-minute break. "When we come back, we'll check out your stickhandling abilities," Coach Flanagan told them as they headed for the bathrooms and the vending machines.

"Hey, Wells, lookin' good out there!" Teddy Chester told him, clapping him on the back.

"Yeah, well," Chris said, flushing as a group of kids congratulated him.

"Too bad it won't do you much good in a hockey game."

"Huh?"

"I'd like to see you skate like that with a pair of defensemen coming at you," Teddy said, and the other kids all laughed. "Mommy! Mommy! He hit me, Mommy!"

Chris felt himself flushing crimson now, and for a different reason than before. They still thought he

39

was a momma's boy! Even though he'd skated better than any of them!

As he sipped on his sports drink, Chris watched the other kids banging playfully into one another. Some were already back out on the ice, passing the puck back and forth.

Suddenly, a chill went up and down Chris's spine. He'd never practiced with a stick and puck! Yesterday, with Lynne, sticks hadn't been allowed on the ice during free-skate. And now, he felt totally unprepared — as if one of his teachers had surprised the class with a test on something he hadn't even studied for.

He grabbed the stick Lynne had borrowed for him and went back out onto the rink. The ice was all chewed up by now, and there were a lot of rough spots. Even the practiced hockey players were having trouble working the puck around. It kept flying into the air, taking weird bounces.

How do those NHL players manage to control the puck so easily? Chris wondered, seeing the kids here struggle with it. He wondered how he would do at this next series of drills, having never even played hockey before. . . .

"All right, we've got Alfonse Ferrugia in goal," Coach Flanagan said. "Alfonse was traveling team MVP last year, and he'll be back in goal again this season. So most of you won't have to try and score off him. Lucky for you guys. Alfonse is tough.

"So here's how it works," the coach went on. "I'll form you up into lines — two wingers and a center. It's like in basketball, a fast-break drill. I wanna see passing — crisp and clean — and I want each line to get off one good shot. Shouldn't be too hard, with no one playing defense. If you're the one with the puck at the right moment, shoot it. Otherwise, pass it off. Okay, here we go."

Chris was put at center, with kids he knew from school — seventh graders like himself — on either wing. Chris started out with the puck, but right away he messed up, allowing the slippery disk to slide off the end of his stick before he could even make his first pass. Coach blew his whistle, and they started over.

The second time, Chris managed to pass the puck, but he sent it behind his right winger and the play was busted before it ever got going. Coach blew his whistle again, and Chris winced as he heard the snickers from the kids who were watching, waiting their turn to skate.

This time, Coach put Chris on right wing. The center passed the puck left, then the left winger sent it back to center. Finally, the puck came Chris's way — and he actually caught it on his stick! There he was, bearing in on the goalie. Should he shoot, or pass back to center? He remembered what Coach had said about taking the shot if you had it.

Alfonse, the goalie, was skating out toward him, cutting off his shooting angle. Chris, panicking, reared his stick back and shot the puck!

Except that the puck was still sitting there — he'd missed it entirely! He'd whiffed the shot. Made a fool of himself. The snickers from the sidelines grew louder, and Chris got more and more embarrassed.

He skated to the sideline and took a seat, watching as other lines took their rushes at Alfonse Ferrugia. Most of their shots were stopped by the goalie, who was amazing. But at least their shots went in the general direction of the net — nobody else whiffed completely, the way Chris had.

The next time up, Chris passed the puck off instead of shooting it — even though he had a clear shot this time. His pass sailed way in front of the center, Teddy Chester, who banged his stick on the ice in frustration. "Come on!" he shouted at Chris, who said, "Sorry," in a small voice.

Next were one-on-one rushes. Chris had the puck slide off his stick, or bounce away, four or five times before he finally got off a weak shot that missed the net by six feet to the right.

Chris felt a large lump growing in his throat. He wanted to get out of here, and find a stall in the boys' room where he could be alone and cry his eyes out. He'd blown this tryout royally — and after such a good start, too!

He skated for the sideline, and the murmurs and snickers were a loud noise in his ears, singing his shame, his total humiliation.

Chris looked up into the stands. All the kids were laughing at him. All but one: Derek Morgan sat scowling as usual, except he wasn't looking at Chris this time — he was looking at all the others.

Derek seemed to hate everything and everybody. Chris was glad he wasn't like that. He didn't hate anybody — not really. Not even the kids who were laughing at him, making whispered comments about what a loser he was. He didn't blame them. He'd probably have done the same in their shoes.

Or maybe not. Chris couldn't imagine himself laughing at somebody else's misery. What was funny about something like that, anyway? People only laughed because they were relieved it wasn't them, because it made them feel like they were better than that other person; that loser — *him*.

Derek Morgan was out on the ice now. He skated in like a freight train, then wound up full and sent a rocket at Alfonse Ferrugia. The goalie ducked from the speeding missile, and it ripped right through the net behind him, thudding against the boards behind the goal!

The murmur in the stands escalated to a roar. Derek turned and skated past them, scowling at them all as he went, as if to say, *I could do that to any of you. All you've gotta do is look at me the wrong way.*

Everyone but Chris looked away, down at their shoes or at the far wall of the rink — anywhere but back into Derek's blazing eyes.

Only Chris looked directly back at him. He

wished he was big and mean like Derek, and could shoot like him. People would never make fun of Derek to his face the way they did to Chris.

"Okay, men," Coach Flanagan said when the try-out was over. "You all did really well. Team rosters will be posted on the bulletin board at the front of the rink by tomorrow afternoon. So you can stop by and see whether you made it, and what team you're on. Traveling Team will be contacted directly by Coach Berman, so don't go bothering him, asking if you made the Screaming Eagles. Like I said, it's very difficult, and only a few of you will be on that team. So that's it. Thanks for coming down, and good luck to all of you."

Chris got out of his padding and uniform and into his street clothes. He went up to Bobby Cosmillo and said, "Here. These are your little brother's. I don't think I'm going to be needing them anymore. Tell him thanks for me, okay?"

Bobby gave Chris a puzzled look, then shrugged. "Whatever you say," he said, taking the stuff from him.

"I mean, I'm not gonna make Town League, so what's the use, right?" Chris said with a sad smile.

45

"You never know," Bobby said, not really interested in talking to Chris. "See ya."

Chris went outside and trudged toward his mom's station wagon, which was parked in the lot with about a hundred other cars. He wondered what he would say to his mom when she asked him how it had gone.

Whew, he thought. *This might be the hardest part of all.*

"So how'd it go?"

"Good."

"Really? That's great!"

"It was okay."

"What do you mean?"

Chris shrugged. "Some good, some bad."

And that was it. No further discussion. His mom didn't ask him if he'd made the league, or when he'd find out, or anything. Chris figured she was probably content to let the whole thing fizzle out without her doing anything.

Lynne wasn't letting him off the hook so easily, though. On the way to school the next morning, she pumped him for information.

"If you really wanted to know, you could have come and watched," Chris said, not wanting to discuss it.

"No I couldn't have," she said. "I was . . . busy."

Chris heard the hesitation in her voice. He wondered what it meant. She hadn't said she'd be there in the first place, so she had no call to feel guilty about not showing up. Maybe it was something else altogether that was bothering her. But he decided not to ask.

They talked about their classes instead. They were in different grades, but Chris had had all Lynne's teachers the year before and could easily understand her frustrations with one or two of them.

The day went by in a fog for Chris. His mind was on hockey, wondering whether or not he'd made the league. He didn't think everybody made it — he was sure not. There'd been over a hundred kids there last night, and it was only one of three nights of tryouts. With only eight teams in the league, and twenty kids on a team, that meant many of the kids would be left off the roster.

After school, he walked straight to the rink — a distance of over a mile, in the opposite direction from his house. He just had to know if he'd made it or not. He didn't care if he had to walk to China and back. He couldn't stand the suspense another minute!

There were the eight sheets of paper, with the eight team rosters. Chris scanned them one by one. He didn't see his name the first time through.

Hmmm, he thought. *Maybe I missed it.*

He looked over the lists again. No. His name was not there. He'd failed the tryout!

Chris felt as if a crushing weight had fallen from the ceiling and landed right on his heart. Seven years of figure skating, and he couldn't even make Town League hockey! What a geek he was! What a total loser!

The other kids had been right to make fun of him, Chris mused as he trudged slowly back home, alone with his miserable thoughts. He *was* a momma's boy. If he'd stood up to her when Dad had left the family, and insisted on playing hockey instead of taking figure skating lessons, he'd have built himself up by now into a bigger, tougher kid.

Now it was too late. He'd never get to play hockey. He'd probably never grow another inch or gain another pound, either.

When he got home, it was already dinnertime. His mom had left a note on the table: "Hi, Honey — dinner is in fridge; breaded tofu cutlets and rice with string beans (must eat!). I'll be back by seven-thirty. Oh, and the hockey coach called, said to call him back any time tonight — 748-6847. Luv u. Mom."

The coach had called! Chris yanked the cordless off its base and punched in the number. "Hello?" came a man's voice.

"Coach? It's Chris Wells." Chris could feel his heart thumping. He wondered if the coach could hear it too — it was that loud. Had he made the team after all? Maybe the coach had left his name off by mistake.

"Yes, hi, Chris. Coach Berman here."

"Coach *Berman?*" The traveling team coach! But why was *he* calling?

"Yes, I run the twelve- and thirteen-year-olds' traveling all-star team. I saw your tryout yesterday, and I'd like you to be a part of it."

Chris thought he was going to pass out right then and there. The traveling team! An all-star! A Screaming Eagle!

Wait a minute.

"Who is this *really?*" Chris demanded, annoyed now.

"It's . . . Coach Berman. Didn't I say that already?"

"Yeah, right. You must think I'm an idiot," Chris said.

"Um, look, young man . . . I don't know what you're thinking, but this is Chuck Berman."

Chris swallowed hard. "Coach?" he asked. "I, um . . . sorry. It's just that, well . . ." He didn't know what to say. Could this really be happening? Or was it just somebody's sick idea of a joke?

He decided to take a chance and play along. "Okay," he said. "Sure, I'll be on the traveling team."

"Well, great! That's great. I was very impressed with your skating ability."

"I have to tell you, though — I've never played hockey before. Never in my life, except once or twice in the street."

The man laughed. "Well, that would explain your stickhandling difficulties," he said. "But we'll work on that with you. I think I can bring you up to speed by mid-season at the latest. And the way you skate, son, you don't need to be a great stickhandler, just adequate."

"Th-thanks," Chris stammered, beginning to

really believe it now. "Gee, I — I don't know what to say. . . ."

"Where'd you learn to skate like that if you never played hockey, anyway?"

"I, um, I took figure skating. Seven years."

"I see. Well, you must be pretty good at it. You had the fastest time ever on a couple of those drills for a twelve- to thirteen-year-old."

"Really?" Chris felt himself swelling with pride. "Um, do I need equipment?"

There was a short silence, as if he'd surprised the coach with his question. "Why, yes, I'm afraid so," he said. "Is that a problem?"

"No! Uh, just . . . like, what exactly do I need?"

The coach had him make a list of all the equipment he'd need and told him to report to practice next Monday at four o'clock.

Chris hung up and braced himself against the countertop, lest his wobbly knees give way underneath him.

The traveling team! He'd bypassed Town League altogether — he was an instant all-star!

"Wait till I tell Mom!" he cried. "Whooo-hoo!"

❖   ❖   ❖

52

He told her as soon as she walked in the door. She congratulated him as warmly as she could. Chris could tell she was proud of him. He could also tell she was worried he might get hurt. Town League was one thing — playing against teams made up of all-stars, most of whom were already thirteen, was another thing entirely.

Still, he had to give her credit. She didn't back off and say no. And when he handed her the list of equipment items he needed, she promised to get off early from her day job at the office to take him shopping after school. Not a word about his dad, Chris noticed. He sure hoped his father was as good as his word for a change.

He showed off his new stuff for Lynne the next day. She was as proud as could be. "I told you I could toughen you up!" she crowed with delight, checking him out in his hockey getup. "You look awesome, like the Terminator!"

"Yeah, well, you can't really see it once you put the uniform over it," Chris said.

"When do they give you one?"

"I hope at first practice!" Chris said. "I don't really have anything to wear otherwise."

"Don't worry," she counseled. "I'll loan you one of my sweatshirts. It'll be plenty big enough to cover your padding."

Chris made a face. "Do you have to remind me?" he complained.

"What? You think I *like* being this tall? Nobody ever asks me out."

"Lynne, you're eleven. Give it time. The guys'll catch up."

Lynne got suddenly quiet.

"What is it?" Chris asked her. "What, is there some guy you like?"

"Shut up!" she told him, snapping out of her funk. "I don't wanna talk about it, anyway. Maybe some other time."

"There is!" Chris said, pointing at her and flashing a mischievous smile. But when he saw how the teasing pained her, he backed off immediately. "Sorry," he said. "It's your business. Um, does he know?"

"Chris!"

"Sorry. Sorry, sorry."

"Anyway, I'm glad you made traveling team."

"Yeah," Chris said, his voice fading to an uncertain tone. "Except . . . well, I don't know if I'm really good enough. I mean, you should have seen me stickhandle. I totally choked."

"Practice in the driveway," she told him. "On roller skates."

"Yeah?" He hadn't thought of that.

"Why not? It's not that different. I've got a net I can loan you." And right there and then, she fished it out of her garage for him.

Over the next few days, Chris spent every after-school hour in his driveway, working on his hockey skills. Gradually, he got used to keeping the puck on the end of his stick. Now he was able to go from end to end of the drive without losing control of it.

He practiced banging into the garage door, too. For years, one of his big goals as a figure skater was never to make contact with the boards. In hockey that was impossible, he knew. He was going to be hitting the boards hard, so he figured he might as well get used to it.

As he played, he let himself dream. He came up with a sportscast inside his head, complete with the cheering crowd and the other sounds of the rink. He ran through entire games in which he came out the hero, carrying the puck end to end and scoring the winning goal in overtime.

Playing with the Screaming Eagles was going to be a blast, he decided. What an honor! How lucky that he'd skipped Town League and gone right to the top!

So when he walked into his first practice, weighted down with equipment, he felt like he was walking into his own dreamscape. Except that before five minutes had passed, the dream began turning into a nightmare.

It started with Chris catching his first glimpse of his new team in action. Out on the ice, players were skirmishing for fun before practice got started. For a moment, Chris thought he'd stumbled into a professional game. These kids were huge! Well, not all of them, but most. He recognized some from school, the eighth-graders.

They were skating, shooting, and hitting each other with intimidating ease. It was hard for Chris to picture himself on the ice with them. He looked like a little kid next to these guys.

On the home-team bench, Coach Berman was talking casually with a group of players. From the way they were bantering back and forth, Chris could tell they'd been together on traveling teams before.

Suddenly, Chris began to wish he'd stuck with Town League. There, he would have had a chance to fit in. Here, he was obviously at the very bottom of the totem pole. His time on the ice would probably be brief, and if he ever saw the puck, it would be totally by accident.

Still, here he was — and if he wanted to stay, he'd better do the best he could to fit in.

"Here!" Chris shouted, stepping out onto the ice and calling for one of the skirmishers to pass it to him.

The kid with the puck looked Chris up and down as if he were from Mars. "Wells? What are you doing here?" It was Teddy Chester — a face Chris had expected to see here, but had conveniently forgotten about.

Teddy's face, under his helmet, lit up in a big grin. With a flick of his stick, he sent the puck winging Chris's way. It hit off Chris's chest and ricocheted away.

"Hey! I wasn't ready," Chris complained. But Teddy had already skated off, laughing, to retrieve the loose puck. Chris rubbed his chest where the puck had hit it. It stung, but what really hurt was getting humiliated like that.

He should have expected it from Teddy, Chris knew. Still, he felt like crying. He bit down hard on his lower lip, determined not to let his emotions show.

"Hey, it's my man Shorty!" Teddy Chester said, skating up to Chris from behind and flinging an arm around his shoulders. "Buddy! It's good to see ya!" he said, shaking Chris roughly back and forth. "Hey, guys, we're gonna be champions this year. We've got Peanut!"

Some of the other kids laughed. Then Coach Berman looked up to see what was going on, and the laughter died down in a hurry.

"Hey, Peanut, lemme introduce you around," Teddy offered in a more sincere tone. "This is Alfonse — you already met him at tryouts. . . ."

"Hey," Chris said, nodding. Alfonse returned it.

"And this is Wikki Withers," Teddy said. A big bruiser skated up to Chris. He reached out a huge hand and patted the top of Chris's helmet like he was patting a pet dog. "He plays defense. Wikki, this is Chris. He's gonna ride the bench."

"He's gonna be the mascot?" Wikki joked. "Hey, a new good-luck charm! Awright!" He gave Chris's helmet another hard rub with his enormous palm.

"You know Jason Chernick?" Teddy went on. "He plays defense, too."

Chris nodded to Jason, whom everybody in school knew. He played sports all year round, and excelled in all of them. A tall, popular eighth-grader who got straight A's, Jason was the kind of kid who made you feel inferior and depressed. Not that he rubbed it in or anything; he didn't need to. He was better than *everybody* at *everything*.

Well, at least I'm better at figure skating, Chris comforted himself.

Coach Berman called the players to attention with a toot on his whistle. "Okay, everybody!" he said. "Welcome back for another great season. Last year, we placed a distant third. This year, we're going to be right up there with the contenders. Pennington's team lost their big two, and Stone Creek lost Kirby, so I think we can compete with both those teams.

"I also want to welcome our new teammates," the coach continued. "We've got three this year who've never been on traveling team before, which is a lot. First, there's Felix Mendez." A tall boy with straight black hair worn in a ponytail stood up and waved shyly to the rest of them.

"Felix is an eighth-grader," Coach Berman went on, "and as you can see, he's big and strong. He's been in Town League for years, but he tells me he grew six inches this year and gained thirty pounds. So Felix will be pairing with Jason Chernick on defense.

"Next, there's Chris Wells." The coach motioned for Chris to wave, which he did. "Chris is a seventh-grader, and he's never played organized hockey before. But he's a heck of a skater, as you'll all soon see. I want everyone to be patient with Chris. He's got a lot of ground to cover before the season starts, and I want us all to help him get there.

"Last but not least . . ." Coach looked around, but didn't see the player he was looking for. "Hmmm, I guess he's not here —"

Just then, they all heard the big steel door at the front of the arena bang open, then shut.

"Ahh," Coach said with a smile. "I believe he's just arrived. Everybody, meet Derek Morgan."

At that precise moment, Derek stepped from the

darkness of the lobby area into the bright lights of the rink. He held up an arm to shield his eyes from the glare and stared into the silence that greeted his arrival.

"*What?*" he called out belligerently. "I'm late, all right? Anybody got a problem with that, we can take it outside."

Nobody did, apparently.

"All right. I'm gonna go get suited up. Be there in a minute."

He left for the locker room, and only when he was gone did the murmur begin to rise.

"What's with him, anyway?" Teddy wondered. "He's got some 'tude, doesn't he?"

Everyone agreed that Derek wasn't exactly sweetness and light. "Maybe he thought Coach was criticizing him," Chris offered.

"What, because he introduced him?" Wikki asked. "Come on."

"You know, at Town League tryouts, everyone was looking at him and pointing at him from the minute he walked in," Chris said. "Maybe they'd never seen a black kid playing hockey before."

They all stopped and looked at him. "Well, you

know what I mean," he went on. "Like when *I* walk in, and everybody starts making jokes about my size."

"Somebody's been making jokes about your size?" Coach Berman asked, frowning.

"No, no," Chris said hurriedly. "I'm just saying, in general . . ." His voice trailed off.

"Well, if I catch anybody making fun of a teammate, for whatever reason, they'll have to answer to me," Coach Berman warned in no uncertain terms.

Derek came back, in uniform and ready to play. Coach Berman then started them off with drills. Chris noticed that everyone played a little shy of Derek. Maybe it was his attitude, or maybe it was just his size, strength, and determination. Whatever it was, Derek made an instant impression. Nobody messed with him. In fact, nobody even *spoke* to him.

For his part, Derek seemed to take this as further evidence of hostility. Drill after drill, his hitting got harder and harder. Eventually, he wound up decking Jason Chernick with a hard hit.

"Hey!" Coach Berman yelled, blowing his whistle. "Back off, Morgan! That was an illegal hit. You know what that means? A five-minute major penalty!"

Skating onto the ice, the coach checked to make sure Jason was okay. Then he turned to the other players. "Look, I don't know what's going on here, but we're all on the same side, okay?"

Jason cast a quick, worried glance Derek's way, then skated away, dusting himself off. Derek stood his ground, he and Coach standing face to face now.

"Look," the coach said, putting his hands out, palms down. "If you've got a problem, why don't you and I talk about it privately?"

"Got no problem," Derek muttered, still casting hard looks at all the other players.

"Good. Then I expect to see that in your play."

"Dang!" Derek spat. Tossing an arm like he was throwing something, he spun and skated off the ice, tramping into the locker room.

Coach Berman stood looking after him, shaking his head. "Oh, boy," he said with a sigh. "He's a tough one."

"Let me talk to him, Coach," Chris volunteered.

The coach eyeballed Chris. "I don't know if that would be a good idea. . . ."

"I think maybe I could calm him down."

Coach sighed. "Well, go ahead then. But if you

run into any resistance, just back off. I think Derek's going through something right now, and maybe he just needs some time to consider his options."

"I'll go easy," Chris promised, and skated off the ice. He thought he knew what was bothering Derek, and he sympathized. People talked about *him* in whispers, too.

"Hey," Chris greeted Derek, who was slumped in front of his locker, staring into space.

"Mmm . . ." Derek didn't turn to face him.

"You okay?"

"What do you care?"

"I dunno. I just do. Listen, Derek, did anybody do anything to offend you in there?"

"Offend me?" Derek turned to him now, glaring. "What makes you think I'd get offended so easily?"

"You're sure acting like it," Chris said simply.

"Well, what do you think it feels like to be the only black person in the whole place? You see any other faces like mine in there, little guy?"

"There, now, see? You just made fun of me for being short!" Chris pointed out.

"It's different."

"Not that different," Chris insisted. "I know how it feels to get made fun of. I mean, look at me!"

"You pretty short, huh?" Derek said, still not smiling. "So what, I'm supposed to feel sorry for you?"

"That's not the point. I just meant you shouldn't be mad. Those guys don't hate you or anything. And Coach was just trying to teach you the rules —"

"Look!" Derek roared, getting up and grabbing Chris's jersey, "I don't need you to be telling me things, okay? Just stay out of my face, yo."

"Okay! Okay," Chris said, freeing himself gingerly and backing out of the locker room.

Whoa! he thought as he stood by the vending machines, waiting for his heart to stop racing. *Excuse me for living.*

Coach had warned Chris not to push Derek. But no, he hadn't listened. And now he'd gone and made the wrong enemy.

So I can tell what's going through this kid's mind," Chris told Lynne the following evening. "He's thinking, 'Everybody hates me, and it's because I'm black.'" He paused, throwing a handful of laying mash to the chicken, who clucked her thanks.

"Do you think he's right?" Lynne asked.

Chris shrugged. "I dunno. Maybe one or two of them are thinking that. More likely, they've just never seen a black kid who played hockey before. I mean, look at the NHL. What do they have, one black hockey player?"

"You know what I think?" Lynne said. "I think it's really important for you to make Derek feel welcome."

"Thanks, but I already tried that. Now he hates my guts. Like he thinks I did it to annoy him."

"You can get past that," Lynne told him. "You've got a good heart. He'll see that sooner or later. Hey, you're the nicest person I know!"

"Thanks," Chris said. Then he frowned and looked at her suspiciously. "Hey, wait a minute. Are you buttering me up for a favor?"

They knew each other so well, after all these years, that the slightest change in Lynne's voice set off alarm bells in Chris's head. Like right now. . . . Lynne was blushing, biting her lip.

"I'm right! I knew it!" Chris accused her.

"Okay, okay," she said, picking up the chicken and hugging it. The chicken opened her red eyes wide, looking at Lynne in confusion. "There's this guy I like. . . ."

"Aha! Didn't I tell you that last time we talked? Yes! I am Svengali! I read your mind! Ha!"

"Shut your face!" Lynne shrieked.

Quickly, Chris backed off, as he always did rather than hurt someone's feelings. "So who is he?"

"Never mind."

"I won't tell. You know I won't. Come on, who?"

"All right. He's on your hockey team —"

"Ugh!" Chris cut in. "Please, don't tell me it's Teddy Chester. I hate him!"

"No, you idiot," Lynne said with a laugh. "His initials are J.C."

"Get out of here! Are you serious? Jason Chernick?"

"Shhhh!"

"Who's gonna hear me, the chicken? Jason! You'd better get in line, there's a lot of girls that like him."

"I know, that's why I need your help. You know, help getting his attention?"

"Lynne," Chris said, "first of all, put the chicken down. I'm getting distracted here. This is a difficult problem."

Lynne put down the chicken, giving it a kiss, which the chicken returned with an affectionate peck. "Okay, I'm listening," she said, turning to Chris.

"I've been to two practices so far, and from what I can see, all he talks or thinks about is sports. If it's not hockey, it's football, or baseball, or soccer, or swimming. What is it exactly you like about him, anyway?"

"He's dreamy."

"Dreamy? Gag me with a spoon."

"Really?"

"No." Chris exhaled sharply. "Okay, look how do you want me to sort of help things along? Want me to ask him if he likes you?"

"No!" Lynne's eyes grew wide with horror. "Are you kidding me? No way!"

"Okay, okay. How about if I just, I don't know, say some nice things about you and see how he reacts?" Chris suggested.

Lynne considered this. "Mmm, okay. But, Chris, go real easy, okay? If he finds out I like him, I'll die of embarrassment, you understand?"

"And I can just imagine what you'll do to *me!*" Chris said, chuckling. "Don't worry. I think I can handle it." Then a funny idea crossed his mind. Chris chuckled again at the thought. "Hey, you know the best way to get his attention?"

"Hmm?"

"Try out for traveling team."

"What!?" Lynne put her hands on her hips and looked at him in stunned surprise. "What are you talking about?"

Chris gave her an amused shrug. "You're a great

athlete. I've seen you play street hockey. You and a goalie against five kids, and you win. So why not?"

"I haven't played street hockey in three years," Lynne reminded him. "Soccer's my sport now."

"Same sport, basically," Chris persisted, the idea actually appealing to him now. "Same basic idea. Same strategy and skills, a lot of the same rules. I repeat, why not?"

"Chris — they don't take girls on traveling team. There aren't that many girls playing hockey at my age, period. There's only two or three of them in the whole Town League!"

"Be the first female traveling all-star!" Chris said, half teasing, half serious. "Just because there hasn't been one doesn't mean there couldn't be one now. And don't tell me, 'Tryouts are over, it's too late.' For a girl, I bet they'd have a special tryout. Nobody wants to get sued, right?"

"Chris, you are such a dummy," Lynne said, dismissing his idea with a little wave of her hand. "But thanks for helping me with You Know Who."

"De nada," he told her. "And think about my idea, huh? I know it's wild, but it sure would get J.C.'s attention."

Of course, it would never happen, Lynne playing for the traveling team. But it sure would be fantastic.

Oh, well. At least Lynne would be there at all the games, rooting him on. He was pretty sure the Screaming Eagles had just found themselves a one-girl cheering section.

At the next practice, after they'd done their warm-up drills, Coach Berman sat them all on the bench for a talk. "All right," he began, "the season's just a few days away. I like what I've been seeing on the ice. Good effort by everybody. But I'd like to see a little more team spirit. I don't want to hear any more criticisms of how somebody is playing."

All eyes went to Chris. He'd been fumbling his stickwork, showing little improvement, and everyone was noticing how far behind the rest of them he was.

"We've got to pull for each other, be there for each other, back each other up, defend each other. That's what champions do, and that's what I expect from you. We need to play hockey like a bunch of brothers. Do you understand me, all of you?"

Now all eyes went to Derek. He hadn't spoken a word to anyone since the moment he arrived, outside of things like, "Yo, heads up." He didn't treat them like brothers — nor they him.

Derek stared down the rest of the team. He was sitting on the far end of the bench, apart from everyone, and did not budge to move himself closer.

At that moment, in that uncomfortable silence, Chris did something he never thought he would do. He got up, sidled over, and sat down next to Derek.

He could feel Derek's anger, and it made him shiver. *Thanks a lot, Lynne,* he thought. *Reaching out sure worked great!*

Coach Berman gave Chris a little nod of appreciation when Derek wasn't looking. "I'm announcing positions today," Coach told the team. "We've got Ferrugia in goal, with Smith in reserve. Chernick and Mendez, first defensive line. Withers and Blake, second defensive line.

"Now for the offense. Line one will be Drake on the right, Milner on the left, and Chester at center." There were whoops and mutual high fives from the best players on the team.

"Second line is Bartlett on the right, Chen on the left, and Young, center." More whoops and high fives. "Third line: Shimaya right, Kendall left, Gold-man center."

Chris shifted uncomfortably, waiting to hear his name. "Fourth line: Morgan right, LaSalle left, Wells center."

Chris let out a little gasp, then swallowed hard. He slowly turned to face Derek.

"You'd better get me the puck at the point, you hear?" Derek's growl was too low for anyone but Chris to hear.

"All right, let's get out there and scrimmage!" Coach said, then blew his whistle.

Chris put on his helmet and grabbed his stick. He needed to lean on it to keep from shaking. This was going to be his biggest test yet. And what would Derek do to him if he failed?

The first two lines went on the ice, facing off against each other. Chris followed Derek down to the end of the bench. They would be next, scrim-maging against the third line.

"Okay, change!" Coach cried after about five min-utes of play. Derek leaped onto the ice and headed for the face-off circle.

"I take all the face-offs," he said. That was more than okay with Chris. Who would want to face off against a guy like Derek? Ricky LaSalle, their left winger, wasn't going to argue.

"Soon as the puck drops, you skate for the blue line," Derek muttered in Chris's ear as the teams formed up. Chris nodded dumbly. The lump in his throat was so big he couldn't speak.

The puck dropped, and Derek's stick was a blur, poking the puck forward down the ice. Chris grabbed it with his stick just outside the blue line, going full speed.

The two defensemen converged on him, but he was past them already. He could see Lyman Smith, the team's spare goalie, coming out to cut him off.

Chris wound up to shoot and slapped at the puck with all his might — except his stick barely touched the puck, which dribbled slowly forward.

But Lyman Smith had been faked out. Seeing the stick whaling like that, he'd dived to stop the shot. The wobbling puck rolled around him, then back toward the net. Jason Chernick, playing defense, reached out with his stick to stop it, but he was too late. The puck died just across the net line. Score!

Chris leaped into the air, shouting. A goal! Yes!

He turned to Derek, figuring at least to get a smile out of him. But Derek's frown stayed put. "Told you I'd get you the puck," he said. "Now this time, I'll send it back the other way. You feed me at the point, like in practice."

"Okay," Chris said. He suddenly realized how lucky he was to be playing on a line with Derek Morgan. It meant he might actually wind up scoring some goals this season. After all, he'd gotten his first goal in about four seconds!

On the second face-off, Chris followed the puck after it was dumped into the zone. He beat Mendez to the puck easily, putting on a burst of speed. Then he passed it straight back to the right point, where Derek was waiting, muscling out Jason Chernick for position.

Derek fired a wrist shot that was as hard as any slap shot Chris had ever seen. Lyman Smith reacted after the puck was already past him — *score!*

"Change lines!" Coach yelled, and Derek and Chris, along with Ricky LaSalle, headed back to the bench.

Coach Berman was looking at Derek, who sat

scowling on the bench drinking a sports drink. The coach's thoughts were as plain as day on his face. He was thinking, *Have I got something good here? A fourth line that plays like a first line?*

Chris felt a jolt of excitement run through him. His goal had been more or less an accident. But that pass he'd made to Derek, and the way he'd gotten to the puck so far ahead of the defenseman, made him think that maybe Coach was right about him. Maybe he did have potential!

Of course, it was only the threat from Derek that had made him play with such focus and desperation. Otherwise, with all the pressure he'd been feeling, he probably would have choked.

Funny how things work, Chris said to himself. Now, thanks to Derek, he'd probably get his chance. Life sure moved in mysterious ways!

Derek got up and sidled down the bench to Chris. He sat down next to him, still scowling — then gave him a hard shove with his hand.

"Hey!" Chris complained, thinking he'd been pushed around.

"Good job," Derek said, his expression never changing.

"Huh?"

"You deaf? I said, 'Good job.' Lucky, but good."

"Oh. Thanks." Chris smiled, but Derek didn't return it.

"I think we play good together," Derek said, staring at the other lines going at it on the ice. "We fit, you know what I'm saying? You're fast, and I'm fast-thinking."

"Uh-huh . . ."

"For instance, I was thinking about what you said the other day."

"What I said . . . ?"

"I decided maybe you're not so wack. Maybe I'm just crazy."

"I didn't say you were crazy."

"I see people lookin' at me, and seein' a black kid, and it's like, 'What's he doin' playing hockey? How come he's not playin' basketball?' So maybe I'm makin' it all up, right? Maybe nobody's thinkin' that but me."

"All I said was, maybe they were looking at you strange because they're scared of you — because you look like you want to beat somebody up."

"I *said* I thought you had a point, all right? I'm

gonna try to give you and all these kids the benefit of the doubt for a while. But don't cross me, understand? I don't take that kind of treatment from anybody."

"Who said you should?" Chris asked.

"I'm just sayin'. Look, I'm gonna concentrate on scoring goals. First game's in two days. You do the same, and we'll be all right. Deal, yo?"

"Deal." Chris nodded, pleased.

"Line change!" Coach shouted.

"Let's go!" Derek shouted, leaping onto the ice, with Chris right behind him.

Chris could feel the butterflies flitting around in his stomach on the morning of the Screaming Eagles' first game. By the time he got to the rink, it felt more like grasshoppers jumping around in there.

Some of his teammates were already at their lockers, putting on their gear. Over in the corner, Jason Chernick was talking with three other players. "You like her?" Alfonse Ferrugia was asking Jason.

"I don't know," Jason said, making a face. "She's kind of, you know, into shopping. I wouldn't know what to talk about with her."

Chris suddenly remembered about Lynne. She'd be up in the bleachers today, he knew, watching the game, screaming and yelling. He edged over to the other boys, pretending to go through his gym bag looking for something, when all he was really looking for was information.

Chris the spy! he thought with a secret smile. He wondered which girl Alfonse was talking about.

"Yeah, but did you see her at the dance?" Wikki was asking.

"So she can dance," Jason said. "So what? I don't even like to dance."

"Man," Felix Mendez said, shaking his head. "All these girls like you, and you don't even pay attention. I don't know how you even concentrate."

Jason chuckled, lacing up his skate. "It's a pain sometimes, to tell you the truth," he said. "Like right now. Do I want to be discussing this? We've got a game in forty-five minutes, duh! Remember what Coach says: Every game's a big game in Traveling League."

"Yeah, yeah," Alfonse said, giving Jason a friendly poke. "This guy's all business. Okay, let's go play, big shot. I expect you to give me some cover today!"

"Count on it," Jason said, high-fiving the goalie.

Dang! The group was breaking up now, and Chris hadn't learned anything much — except maybe that Jason didn't like anybody special, and that all he thought about was sports, which Chris had already guessed.

Alfonse, Felix, and Wikki had already left the locker room and gone to warm up. Chris opened his locker and started getting suited up.

"Man!" Jason said, shaking his head. "Can you believe those guys? That's all they think about is girls. They'll be waving to some babe in the stands, and they'll get hit in the coconut with a puck 'cause they're not looking!"

Chris laughed along with him. Then, on a sudden impulse, he said, "There's this girl I know. I was trying to talk her into trying out for the team."

"For *our* team?"

"Yeah. I was just kidding around. She didn't take me seriously. She said they'd never had a girl on any traveling team. But then I thought, 'Why not?'"

"Never happen," Jason said dismissively. "She could play Town League, maybe, but they'd never let her in here."

"She taught *me* to play," Chris said. "Not that I'm Wayne Gretzky, but I'm telling you, she's good."

"Yeah, well, there's good and there's *good*, know what I mean?"

"I guess. You should see her play, though. She decked me with a few checks."

"Yeah? What's her name?" Jason asked. His interest had definitely perked up.

"Lynne St. James."

"Don't know her," Jason said.

"She's here watching."

"Yeah? Your girlfriend, huh?"

"Not really," Chris said, grinning. "Just a friend. Hey, we'd better get out there."

There. He'd gotten across a key piece of information. And he'd conveniently forgotten to mention that Lynne was still not quite twelve. Way too young for a thirteen-year-old like Jason, in Chris's humble opinion.

He clumped through the locker room and out onto the ice. Looking up into the stands, he could see Lynne spreading her jacket out to make herself comfortable on the hard bleacher seat.

Chris let out a loud whistle — the one she'd taught him — and Lynne looked up. Chris flashed her a thumbs-up, jerking his head toward Jason. Lynne beamed, blushing, and rocked her fists excitedly.

Just then, the other team burst onto the ice, like a

yelling, scary mob. It was a gesture designed to intimidate, and for a second, Chris found himself startled. Looking around, he saw that his teammates had stopped skating and were standing around, watching the Pennington Tigers, last year's champs, go through their warm-ups.

Then, just as suddenly, Derek Morgan stepped onto the ice. He skated right into the middle of the Tigers' warm-up circle. The Pennington players had to dodge to avoid hitting Derek, and the skating circle backed up, causing a traffic jam. Derek just stood there, leaning on his stick, glaring at the visitors.

Now it was the other team's turn to back off, intimidated. Chris and his mates flashed big grins at each other. Derek had shown those other kids who was tougher! Clearly, the Screaming Eagles were glad scrimmages were over. No more playing against Derek. He was now on *their* side for the season.

Coach Berman called the Screaming Eagles over to the bench. "Okay," he said. "Here goes. Remember, in Traveling League, every game's important. It's a short season, and we only get one crack at each of these teams. So ready or not, it's time to go for it. I want to see every one of you going full out all the time. Don't leave anything for tomorrow. All right, put your hands in here."

He put his hand out. Everyone on the team put his hand in. Derek waited until his would be on top.

"Yeah!" they all yelled, throwing their hands into the air. "Go, Eagles!"

The game began. Chris squirmed on the bench as the first three lines took their turns. Things weren't going so well, and Chris found himself gripping the rail with both hands, shouting for the defense to pick up the slack.

Jason Chernick blocked one shot, then Alfonse Ferrugia made a spectacular save. The fans in the stands erupted, and a groan went up from the visitors' side.

"Change! Line four!" Coach yelled, and Derek, Chris, and Ricky LaSalle hopped onto the ice for their first face-off. Derek lined up, glaring at the opposing player, who seemed to cringe for a moment. It was no surprise to Chris when Derek won the face-off, dishing the puck to the defense and starting the Screaming Eagles' first good rush of the game.

Chris sped across the blue line after Derek, trailing in at center. Derek saw him and passed him the puck. Chris slapped at it and diverted it right at the corner of the net.

The Tigers' goalie threw his arm out, and the end of his stick batted the puck away at the last moment. Now it was the Eagles and their fans' turn to groan. The score remained 0–0 at the end of the first period.

"Nice rush, line four," Coach told them as they came back to the bench for a breather between periods. "Their goalie's tough, but we can crack him. Shoot low. He seems to be ready for the high shot."

Everyone nodded, very serious now. If any of the veteran players thought this season was going to be a walkover, they didn't think so anymore. Traveling all-star teams were just that — teams full of good players. Every victory was going to have to be earned.

By the end of the second period, the game was still scoreless. Most of the Eagles looked winded, but Chris didn't feel that way at all. His figure skating had given him great endurance. He was probably in better physical shape than any of them!

Derek didn't look tired, either. He came over to

Chris as the third period was about to start and said, "Look for me at the point. When I wind up, get ready to deflect the shot with your stick."

Chris nodded, although it seemed far-fetched to him. He knew NHL players deflected shots in midair, but *him?*

When their line took the ice, the puck was already scooting along the boards toward the opposing net. Chris took it on his stick and sped down the middle. As he crossed the blue line, he left the puck behind him for Derek, who swooped in for the shot.

Bam! The crack of the stick on the puck was deafening. It didn't sound like anybody else's shot. When Derek Morgan hit the puck, it really got slammed!

Nobody saw the shot. Chris stuck his stick into the air, and felt the puck graze it — but he really didn't see it deflect into the net. The only thing he saw was his teammates leaping into the air.

They'd done it! They'd scored a goal, exactly like Derek had planned it!

On the bench again as play continued, Derek said, "You and me, we've got it going, little man!" Then he grinned — the first time Chris had ever seen him do that. Chris couldn't help smiling back.

When Derek smiled, it was like the sun breaking out after a thunderstorm.

"We gonna score another one today?" he asked Chris.

"You bet!" Chris said, beaming from ear to ear.

Just then, the other team scored a goal, trickling one by Alfonse on a rebound, and the score was tied, 1–1. Chris stopped smiling. "Okay," he told Derek. "Let's go do it."

Derek won the face-off, as usual, then sent the puck into the Tigers' end.

Chris knew the routine. He was after it like a rocket, getting there before the defenseman, then twisting out of the way before he got slammed into.

Ricky had the puck now, and was maneuvering for position. "Over here!" Derek bellowed. Instantly, Ricky passed it off to Derek, who was already into his windup.

Thwack! The shot flew at the goalie, then past him into the net before the poor kid could even react. Score! 2–1, Eagles!

Chris skated back to the bench, his fists high in the air. The game was almost over — all they had to do now was hold on for another minute and a half.

After the next face-off, the Tigers pulled their goalie and sent an extra attacker out onto the ice. "Uh-oh," Chris murmured. "Come on, defense!"

One of the Tigers wound up and took a shot. Jason Chernick dove to block it — and the puck ricocheted right off his helmet!

Jason lay on the ice, motionless. The ref's whistle blew, and all the adults ran gingerly onto the ice to see if Jason was okay. Chris looked up at Lynne in the stands. Her hands were covering her mouth, and her eyes had a look of horror in them.

Luckily, after a few scary moments, Jason sat up. Soon he was being helped off the ice, saying, "I'm okay, I'm okay," in a woozy voice.

Play resumed, but now the heart had been taken out of everybody on both sides. A few seconds later, the final whistle blew. The Eagles exchanged hugs and high fives, shook hands with the Tigers, and quickly headed back to the locker room to check on Jason.

Chris stopped dead in his tracks at the locker room doorway. Jason was sitting on one of the benches, with an ice pack being held to his head by — who else — Lynne! She gave Chris an embarrassed but pleased glance, then turned her attention back to being Jason's nurse.

Jason seemed to not even notice her. He had a goofy grin on his face as he sat there, smiling at his teammates' jokes about using his head. Everyone seemed happy, basking in the glow of the team's first, hard-won victory.

"Hey, good game." Chris turned and saw Derek smiling at him, his hand outstretched. Chris took it and they did a little trick handshake. "You a good little player, dog."

"Thanks. You were awesome today. The look you gave those guys when you first walked in!" The two of them shared a laugh, remembering.

"Yeah, I guess my 'tude's good for something after all," Derek joked. "Listen up, you wanna come over my house for dinner this week? My mama makes some food that'll fatten you up in a hurry. You're way too thin, you know what I'm sayin'?"

"Okay," Chris said, accepting the invitation. "Lemme know when."

"Ayiight." Derek turned to go.

"Hey, Derek —"

"Mmm?"

"You're not as bad as you make yourself out to be."

"That's what you think."

"It *is* what I think. I also think no one else is as bad as you make them out to be."

"That's where you're wrong, my man," Derek said, getting serious in a hurry. "You'll see. Before this season is over, things are gonna happen. Mark my words. And when they do, you better have my back, understand?"

"Sure thing," Chris promised. "Count on it."

"That's my little guy. And don't worry. We're gonna fatten you up, yessiree. You're gonna be one big dude by the time my mama and me get through with you. Ha!"

"Have some more of those lamb chops, Chris!" Derek's mother urged him. "Don't you like them?"

Chris put both his hands on his bulging stomach. The remains of five lamb chops lay piled on his plate. "Yes, ma'am, they were fantastic, but —"

"Look at that boy!" Derek's mom told her son, chuckling. "He looks like he's about to pop out at the seams! Ha!"

"Gotta fatten him up, Mama," Derek said, taking the platter of chops and holding it out to Chris.

"No, no, really, I couldn't," Chris protested weakly. "Really, they were the best I've ever tasted."

"Well, maybe you could take some home in a bag and have them for a midnight snack," Derek's mom suggested. "What does that mama of yours feed you, anyhow?"

"Um, we're vegetarians," Chris mumbled.

"Say what?"

"Vegetarians," he repeated, louder this time.

"But — but you just ate my lamb chops, didn't you?"

"Well, yeah," Chris said with a shrug. "When we eat at people's houses, we eat whatever's served."

"Vegetarian!" Derek's mother repeated, shaking her head. "That's fine for folks who are fat, or have to be on a restricted diet. But look at you! You need to put on some pounds! How're you gonna do that on a bunch of veggies?"

Chris smiled and shrugged. "My mom says vegetarians live longer and healthier. She showed me the statistics and everything."

"Well, I'll be," Derek's mom said. She was a big woman herself, although not really overweight. More like Derek — strong and powerful. "I guess she's right. She's your mama, so you listen to her. But you just come over to my place every once in a while and have some pork chops or ribs, understand?"

"Yes, ma'am!" Chris said enthusiastically.

"Now, I've got an apple cobbler warming up. You want some now, or after a while?"

"I guess I'd better take a break," Chris said. "It smells good, but I need to digest all this food first."

"Come on," Derek said, getting up. "I'll show you my digs."

He took Chris upstairs. "Man," he said as he ushered his guest into his room. "I'm not coming over your house for dinner after any games. Vegetarian food!" He made a noise and shivered in distaste.

"It's good, if you want to know the truth," Chris said. "Not like your mother's cooking, maybe, but my mom's good at sauces and stuff. That's not the reason I'm small. I just haven't hit my growth spurt yet."

"Uh-huh," Derek said, unconvinced.

Chris looked around the room. Plastered all over the walls were posters of hockey greats. Gretzky, Messier, Bure. "Hey, Derek," Chris said. "I'm kinda curious. I hope you won't get insulted by my asking, but how did you get interested in hockey?"

Derek shot him a hard look, but then seemed to decide that Chris didn't mean anything by it. "I used to watch the games on my little TV here after lights out," he confessed with a grin. "It was the only thing on that was any good at that hour."

He stared at Chris. "You wanna know why I don't play basketball, right?"

"I wasn't thinking about that," Chris said honestly. "But since you brought it up . . ."

"Don't tell anybody this, or I'll make you pay, man. I can't jump."

"What?"

"Lookie here." Derek jumped, reaching for the ceiling light. He got about eight inches off the ground, and that was all. "You ever see a worse jump? It's embarrassing."

Chris grinned, then jumped, easily touching the light.

"Oh, man," Derek said with a wince. "How do you do that?"

"Figure skating," Chris told him. "Good for jumping. You should try it sometime."

"Yeah, right, I'll try it, ayiight," Derek said sarcastically. "Anyway, it's a secret, and you'd better keep it."

"I will," Chris promised.

Derek grinned. "I can't dance, either. What you think about that?"

"So there you are," Chris said, turning his palms upward. "Just goes to show you, you can't go by stereotypes."

"My man!" Derek said, slapping Chris five. "Ayiight. We gonna do a victory dance one of these days, though!"

"You got that right!" Chris said. "I could show you how to dance, if you want. I do a lot of it for figure skating."

"Nah, I don't have any rhythm. Anyway, you probably don't listen to my kind of music."

"I perform to Sistah Fudge, Flim-Flamma, and Mo' Money Monique," Chris told him. He laughed as Derek's eyebrows shot up.

"You like hip-hop?" he asked.

"Uh-huh. It's phat," Chris said.

"Yeah," Derek said with a grin. "It's phat. Come here, let me show you my CD collection. You ever hear Spinmaster Steve? Listen here . . ."

Later, after three pieces of Mrs. Morgan's delicious apple cobbler, Chris waddled over to the front door, ready to go. "So after our next victory, you've gotta come over to my house for dinner," he told Derek.

"Oh, no! I told you, I'm not eatin' any of that wack veggie stuff!" Derek said.

"Derek!" his mother scolded him. "That boy's being nice enough to invite you over for dinner. You don't say no. You go, and you clean your plate, and you tell his mama how good her cookin' is, you hear me?"

"Yes, ma'am," Derek said, bowing to a higher authority.

"It's not bad," Chris assured him. "And it's healthy for you. It'll help you jump higher and dance better."

"Very funny, bro. Hey, I'll tell you what," Derek said. "We keep winning games, I'll eat the tires off your mama's car, ayiight?"

The next game was on Saturday morning. Chris's mom had to get him up at six, because the team was riding over to Belleville in a bus. A small group of family and friends were also coming along — among them, Lynne St. James.

She sat with two of her girlfriends, pretty much ignoring Chris, which was fine with him. He didn't want the guys to think he had a girlfriend who was so much bigger than him. And besides, he didn't want Jason Chernick to get the wrong idea, just in case he liked Lynne back.

Lynne paid no attention to Jason, either, but Chris caught her glancing over at him every once in a while. As for Jason, he was busy talking hockey with Alfonse and Wikki. Jason was going to try to play today, but Coach Berman had already said he wasn't putting him out on the ice unless the game was on the line. No sense risking another hit to the head so soon after the last one.

Next to Chris sat Derek. It was way cool to be friends with the hottest player on the hockey team, Chris thought. No longer were they made fun of. Not after last week's game. They sat there and talked about strategies and how they were going to take it to the other team, the Belleville Bulls.

"You think if we score again today, Coach will move us up to third line?" Chris wondered.

"If he doesn't," Derek said, scowling, "it'll be because you're skinny and short and I'm black."

"Cut it out," Chris scoffed. "Don't even go there. Let's just score a goal and see what happens."

✿   ✿   ✿

They didn't score a goal that day. They scored four. Or, to be more precise, Derek scored four, two of them assisted by Chris, one by Ricky. The second goal was a beautiful breakaway in the second period, when the score was still tied at 1–1. Derek simply took the puck off the stick of the Bulls' forward and skated in alone on the goalie.

His shot was so intimidating, his yell so bloodcurdling, that the goalie couldn't help but cringe, closing his eyes as the shot zipped toward him. The poor kid never even saw it go past him and into the net.

After his first goal, Derek got a few pats on the back. But after the breakaway, and on each of the goals after that, all his teammates mobbed him. He was their new hero, a bona fide all-star, and the flat-out best player on the Screaming Eagles.

And I'm his best friend on the team, Chris thought proudly, as they lined up to shake hands with the other team when it was all over.

The fans were waiting at the bus to greet them after they'd showered and changed. Lynne hugged Chris, squealing and jumping up and down. "You were so great! You were all so great!" she kept saying.

Coach Berman looked happy, too. "I think we've

got us a winner this year!" he kept saying to the family and friends of his players. "I'm real proud of the way they played today. Six–one over a team of all-stars is not easy!"

"MVP! MVP! MVP!" some of the players were shouting, raising Derek's arms over his shoulders. It made Chris happy to see Derek so totally accepted and respected. He knew it would help Derek's mood, keeping him on the sunny side of the street. As long as they kept winning, and Derek kept scoring, everything was going to go like a dream.

Chris noticed that Lynne was working her way through the crowd of players, edging her way closer to Jason Chernick. "Great game!" she told him, giving him a quick, embarrassed hug.

Jason stared at her blankly. "Yeah, thanks," he said, though he'd only played for a couple of shifts, just to get out there and feel the game again. "Um . . ."

"Lynne. Lynne St. James. I was holding the ice pack to your head last week, remember?" Lynne's face looked hopeful yet pained.

"Oh. Yeah," Jason said, obviously lying. "I was kind of out of it, I think."

"Huh. Yeah!" Lynne laughed, too hard and too long. Finally, she tore herself away from Jason and boarded the bus, her face beet red.

Poor Lynne, Chris thought. *He doesn't even know she's alive. The only thing Jason Chernick thinks about is sports. She can't possibly compete.*

Chris felt sorry for her. Having a crush on somebody was a real pain in the neck, as far as he was concerned. He wondered if he should counsel Lynne to give it up. He decided not to, though. It was her business, and she had to go through it her way.

All the way back to Cedarville, he tried to figure out a way to help. "Come on, I'll walk you home," he told her as they got off the bus in front of the rink.

Lynne followed him silently, deep in her thoughts. He let her be, not saying anything. But the silence was louder than anything he could have said.

The flag was up on Lynne's mailbox. She opened the box and took out a letter. "It's for me, from the Parks and Recreation Department." She tore open the envelope.

"What? What is it?" Chris asked.

"Yes! I got in!" She turned to him, her eyes wet with happiness. "I made Town League!"

"Huh? I didn't even know you tried out!"

"Yeah, after we talked that time, I decided, you know, what the heck? So they gave me a special late tryout, because I'm a girl and they didn't want to get sued or something. And I made it!"

Then her smile faded. "Of course, it doesn't really matter. . . ." And just like that, she was back into her funk.

Chris sighed. He knew how she had to be feeling. What did it matter to Lynne that she'd made Town League? It wasn't like she'd made the Screaming Eagles. Jason still wasn't going to notice her. And to a girl like Lynne, under the weight of a heavy crush, nothing else was going to matter.

What'd you say this is made of?" Derek was holding a jiggling white cube on his fork, regarding it warily.

"Bean curd," Chris's mom told him. "Try it, it's really quite good." She smiled, waiting for him to eat the quivering morsel.

Derek squeezed his eyes shut and popped the white cube into his mouth. "Mmmm!" His eyes popped back open. "This *is* good!"

"Man, I can't believe you've never had tofu before!" Chris said, giggling.

"Have you had fried okra?" Derek turned on him with a playful scowl. "I'm gonna make you eat that next time you come over for dinner. And pig's feet. Yeah, that's the ticket."

Chris laughed again.

"The secret of tofu," his mom told Derek, "is that it picks up the flavor of whatever you cook it with. So it can taste like anything!"

"That's cool," Derek acknowledged. "I'm gonna tell my mama about it. And you say it's healthy, huh?"

"Everything my mom serves is healthy," Chris told him, winking at his mother. *"Everything."*

"I don't hear you complaining," his mom said with a smile. "Well, I'm so glad to meet you, Derek. I understand everyone in town wants to have you over for dinner these days."

"Yes, ma'am," Derek said, smiling. "I've got a few new friends I don't even know."

"That's 'cause everybody knows you now," Chris told him. "Nine goals in three games, we're three and oh, and you've got half our team's goals!"

"A man from the town paper called me yesterday," Derek informed them. "He said they're gonna write something about me. I told him it better not say 'black hockey player' or anything like that. I'm a hockey player like everybody else, that's all."

"Some kind of hockey player," Chris said, patting him on the back.

"Hey, man, you assisted on most of those goals.

That's just as important. I don't see anybody comin' after you to put you in the paper, or invite you over to dinner."

"You invited me," Chris reminded him.

"That doesn't count," Derek said, frowning. "Hockey's a team game. Gotta honor the team."

"The stands were pretty full the other night," Chris said, changing the subject. "I hear they're going to have a second bus when we travel to White Lake."

"That right? Man!" Derek said, looking pleased. "Yeah, I like it!" He slapped Chris five, then turned to Mrs. Wells. "Ma'am, I appreciate the good dinner. Everything was fine."

"Why, thank you, Derek," Chris's mom said as the boys got up. "You two go on, I'll clean up."

"Sure we can't help?" Derek asked her.

"Sure I'm sure. Such a polite boy!" she gushed to Chris. "Go on, now. I think somebody's waiting to see you next door."

Lynne had made Chris promise to bring Derek over after dinner. He led his friend across the driveway and through the gate that led to the St. James family zoo.

Lynne was carrying the bunny when she saw them. "Hey!"

"Hey, Lynne." Chris waved. "You remember Derek?"

"Sure!" Lynne put the bunny down, attached its long leash to a spike stuck in the ground, and came over to shake hands.

"Oh, yeah, you're the girl who's always yellin' in the stands!" Derek said, grinning as he recognized her.

"That's me!" Lynne beamed.

"Lynne made Town League!" Chris bragged on her, causing Lynne to blush.

"That right?" Derek asked, impressed.

Just then, out walked the chicken, casting a wary red eye at Derek and clucking plaintively.

"You got a chicken!" Derek gasped. "Ayiight! My granddaddy had a chicken market in Lakewood when I was growin' up."

"Really?" Lynne asked, picking up the chicken and exchanging a little kiss with it. "This is Buc-Buc. She knows her name. You just call her — 'Buc-Buc Chicken!' — and she comes running."

"Yeah, chickens are funny," Derek agreed. "I re-member once when Granddaddy cut one of 'em's head off, it was runnin' around without it for a looong time."

"Eeeuuww!" Lynne cried. She dropped the chicken and it flapped its wings, floating to the ground in a huff. Lynne's hand went to her mouth, her eyes grew wide, and her face started getting distinctly green. She looked like she was going to barf any second.

Apparently, Derek thought this was all pretty hysterical. He was laughing his head off at the memory, oblivious to Lynne's discomfort. "Yeah, boy, that was phat! That chicken just kept goin' and goin', like the rabbit in the commercial."

"Derek," Chris warned him, "chill, okay?"

"Huh?"

"Just chill." He indicated Lynne with a nod of his head.

"Oh. Sorry," Derek said, his laughter ebbing slowly. "It was just so funny . . ."

"Chickens dying is not funny," Lynne muttered.

"Huh! You say she plays Town League hockey?" Derek asked, looking Lynne up and down.

"Yeah," Chris confirmed.

"That right?" Derek seemed surprised. He shook

his head. "I don't know. I don't think she's tough enough for hockey. Maybe she oughta play golf or croquet or something instead."

"You take that back!" Lynne screamed, lunging at Derek and grabbing his shirt with both hands. Her face was inches from his, and the whites of Derek's eyes showed all around.

"Whoa!" he gasped, totally stunned. "Ayiight, I take it back, yo! I didn't mean anything by it, know what I'm sayin'?"

Lynne let him go with a little shove. Chris looked on, wide-eyed and silent.

"I scored two goals in my first game, for your information," she told Derek. "I'd go head to head with you, no problem." She looked Derek up and down with a sneer. "I could handle you." Turning on her heels, she stormed up the back steps and into her house.

Derek nodded slowly, and a sly smile spread across his face. "Ayiight, I guess I was wrong. She's tough enough at that."

Game four was another laugher, 8–3 in favor of the Screaming Eagles. Game five was even more spectacular — an 11–2 thrashing of the Wood-bourne Wolves. During that rout, Derek had actu-ally set up Chris for two goals of his own. Chris's stickhandling was coming along nicely now, mostly because in between games Derek was dragging him out to the rink to practice.

Chris had even developed a decent wrist shot, which meant that the more the other teams keyed on Derek, the more Derek could dish the puck to Chris for the quick wrister.

Coach Berman had made them the number-one line after game three, an obvious move since they had accounted for more than half the team's scoring total. Even their linemate, Ricky LaSalle, had scored a goal on the line's big spree.

Meanwhile, on defense, Jason Chernick was play-ing like an all-star. So was Alfonse Feruggia, who had started the season as the team's most likely MVP candidate.

Of course, that distinction now belonged to Derek. The newspaper article in the *Cedarville Gazette* had called him a "hockey phenom," and Derek soon found that he couldn't walk down the street without people waving and calling out encouragement to him.

Derek had begun to smile on a regular basis, which Chris thought was pretty amazing, considering that at first he'd barely ever smiled at anybody! Everybody wanted to be Derek's best buddy. Chris had become popular, too, just by being Derek's friend.

Chris had now eaten dinner three times at the Morgan house, and he could almost feel himself getting bigger and heavier. He couldn't tell if he'd grown any, because he and his mom had not kept up the family custom of marking his height on the wall. That had stopped after his dad moved out.

If there was one sore spot in Chris's life, it was that his dad hadn't even called to see how the team was doing. Chris tried to come to terms with the fact that his dad would probably never see him play hockey. Well, at least he had company in that department. Derek's dad, it turned out, had left the family, too. Derek never spoke with him and didn't even know where he was.

Chris didn't know which was worse — having a

dad who'd abandoned the family, or having one who'd died, like Lynne's father. Chris really envied those kids whose dads came to the games to cheer them on.

But at least Chris was having fun these days. He'd had more good times playing hockey these last six weeks than he'd had in the last three years of figure skating.

Now that he was starting to be popular, he thought he could probably go back to figure skating after the hockey season without getting made fun of for it. Yes, he might just do that. He could picture having fun skating solo again, now that he'd played some hockey. Being on a team was awesome — especially a great team like the Screaming Eagles!

The day finally came for the last game of the regular season. Chris was relaxed as he got into the car with his mom for their drive to the rink. "Excited?" she asked him.

"Yeah," he said. "But sad, too, because the season's practically over."

"Well, aren't you going to be in the championship game, no matter what happens today?"

"Yeah. We're six and oh, and so's the team we're

playing. Both of us are already in, so this is kind of like a rehearsal for the championship game. Still, it's almost over."

"You going back to figure skating afterward?" she asked him.

"Well, Town League plays for another month, so I might transfer over. Lynne says her team has an opening. It would be cool to play with her."

"I think it's so wonderful that she made the team," his mom said.

"I saw her game last week. She goes after the puck really strong."

"Mmm-hmm . . ."

"Anyway, I might go back to figure skating after that."

They were near the rink already. Cars were lined up all the way to the parking lot, along with two of the visiting team's buses. Apparently, both unde-feated teams had their legions of fans wanting to see whose winning streak would survive.

"Just drop me off here, okay?" Chris asked his mom as they passed in front of the arena.

"Sure, honey. See you inside. Oops! Wait a minute — where's my good luck kiss?"

Chris leaned over and kissed her. "In case I forgot to tell you, Mom: Thanks for letting me play hockey."

She beamed with pleasure and pride. "I'm glad I did," she said.

A group of players wearing yellow jerseys and carrying equipment bags was crowding the entrance to the arena, barring Chris's progress. He stood there, waiting impatiently. He wanted to get inside and suit up, to be one of the Screaming Eagles again, for the second-to-last time this year.

Not only had he been accepted by his teammates, he'd become totally one of them, an essential member of an undefeated team. For Chris, it was a dream come true. It was one of the few times in his life when everything had worked out just the way he'd imagined it.

"Don't mess with me, Regan!" an angry voice ahead of him cried. Chris saw the speaker shove another boy, who was wearing the same yellow uniform as his attacker.

"Nuts to you, Chevy."

"You're a wimp, Regan."

"Shut up, you dweeb!" said Regan, leaping at the

boy named Chevy. Other boys wearing yellow jerseys tried to separate them, yelling at them to cut it out. "Lay off me, Chevy," Regan replied. "Nobody calls me that."

"Sorry, I didn't mean it," Chevy said unconvincingly. Two other yellow-jerseyed boys had his arms and were literally bending him to their will, twisting just as hard as they needed to.

Chris's jaw dropped. He'd never seen two teammates go at each other like that. Okay, there had been arguments among the Eagles during practice, but never in front of outsiders! Certainly, before a big pride game like this, a team ought to hang together. The Eagles ought to have no trouble beating a team like this one, whose members argued among themselves.

And yet, Chris could feel the goosebumps rising on his arms and neck. There was something creepy about the hardness of those two boys. He actually felt *afraid* of them. What a bunch of thugs!

Chris knew the Stone Creek Avalanche, last year's runners-up, were 6–0, just like the Eagles. Was this the secret to their success? Had they simply scared the other teams into submission?

"Well, I'm gonna trash talk him," Chevy said to Regan as his teammates turned him loose, "whether you do or not. Gonna make him throw the first punch."

"Go ahead," Regan replied, nonchalant. "After he decks you, I'll be there to pick you up off the ice."

Chris wondered who they were talking about, but he never got the chance to find out. The yellow jerseys passed through the door into the arena, and now it was Chris's turn. He went inside and headed for the boys' locker room (the visiting team got the girls' locker room, which some of the guys thought of as a joke on the opposition).

"Hey, guys!" he greeted his teammates, most of whom were already suiting up. They let out a yell of greeting, making Chris break out into a big smile. Yup. He was home here, and these were his guys. Man, he loved hockey!

"Derek, hey," he said, slapping his friend on the arm.

"Ayiight!" Derek smiled back, nodding. "We're gonna beat these dudes into the ground, dog!"

"Hoo, hoo, hoo!" the team chanted in agreement. Everybody was totally psyched. Chris could feel the electricity himself. The Eagles were going to come out flying. Everyone wanted to beat the Avalanche.

But as they skated onto the ice for the opening face-off, Chris could feel the goosebumps rising again. The yellow-jerseyed kids were casting menacing looks at him, and at all the other Eagles.

Chris wasn't imagining it — there was definite malice in their eyes. Something was up. Something was going to go down, he could feel it in the air. . . .

Suddenly, it happened. As Chevy skated by Derek, circling him to get to the face-off circle, he knocked into Derek's shoulder from behind.

"Hey! Yo!" Derek shouted immediately.

"Oops!" Chevy said, his voice dripping with sarcasm. "Sorry."

"Yeah, you're gonna be sorry!" Derek shouted at him, throwing his stick to the ground.

A murmur went up from the crowd as Derek skated toward Chevy. Luckily, the referee skated between them and held Derek off.

"There'll be no fighting!" he shouted. "No funny business, understand? I don't want anybody getting hurt, and any hard checks will be penalized. No excuses!" He let go of Derek, who brushed off his uniform, simmering as he stared at Chevy.

Chevy turned away, a smirk of victory on his face. Derek looked at Chris. "You see?" his eyes were saying. "Didn't I tell you something like this would happen before the season was over?"

Chris wanted to tell Derek that it wasn't just him, that these were just rough kids, not necessarily racists. But something told him Derek might be right this time. . . .

The game began with Derek taking the face-off from the boy named Regan. Ricky LaSalle took the puck and sent it down-ice, and Chris was off like a shot, digging the puck out of the corner. He reached it before the defenseman and flipped it out in front of the goalmouth.

Derek was already there, crashing into the crease. But the Eagles were playing a good team today — an undefeated team. The Avalanche goalie made a spectacular save with his leg pad, nearly doing a somersault to stop Derek from scoring.

The puck bounced out in front, and Chevy grabbed it with his stick and took off down the ice. Chris was out of position, unable to help as Chevy skated past Jason Chernick, who had come up during the rush. Chevy was so fast on his skates that Jason never had a chance.

But Derek, incredibly, was staying with him, dogging him from behind with his outstretched stick. Chevy got off a pretty good shot, but not good enough to get past a sliding Alfonse Ferrugia. Chevy slammed into the net, knocking it off its pins and causing the ref to stop play with his whistle.

During the lull, Chris saw Chevy skate up to Derek and whisper something in his ear. Derek scowled, then took a quick jab at Chevy with the point of his stick. Chevy ducked out of the way, but the ref had seen the gesture. "Hey!" he yelled at Derek. "Watch the stick, kid. You try that again, it's a major penalty, understand?"

Derek was biting his lip hard to keep himself from protesting. Chris could see that his friend was fuming with anger. He wondered what Chevy had said to make Derek that angry.

"Line change!" Coach Berman called out before the puck was dropped. Obviously, he'd seen what was going on and wanted to keep Derek from exploding.

On the bench, Coach came over to them. "What happened?" he asked Derek.

"Nothing," Derek muttered darkly.

"He say something to you?"

"Uh-huh."

"What?'

"Nothin'."

"Look," Coach said, putting a hand on Derek's shoulder. "Don't pay any attention to that garbage. Why should you lower yourself and get down in the gutter with a kid like that?"

Derek said nothing.

"You want me to speak to their coach?" Coach Berman asked.

"Nuh-uh."

"You sure?"

"Uh-huh."

"Well, okay . . . but you stay out of trouble, you hear? We need you." Coach glanced out at the ice. "Line change!" he shouted again.

On their next turn, Chevy struck again. This time, Chris heard Chevy's comment: "What happened? You couldn't make the basketball team?"

Derek totally lost it. All at once, his stick had dropped to the ice and his fists were flying, flailing away at Chevy, who was covering up, not punching back. The ref's whistle blew loud and clear. Chris and the others had to pry Derek off Chevy, who emerged from his protective position with a nasty grin on his face.

Now, too late, Chris realized that this had been Chevy's plan all along — this was what he'd been trying to talk Regan into! They must have heard about Derek Morgan — about his talent and his temper — and they were going to try to lure Derek into the penalty box, where he couldn't hurt them!

Why hadn't he warned Derek about it? Why, oh why, hadn't he told him what he'd heard Chevy saying about trash talk? Chris felt like kicking himself as he sat back down on the bench. He was not a part of the penalty killing team, which was made up of the biggest, strongest players the Eagles had.

Derek was sitting in the penalty box, banging his forehead repeatedly with the butt of his stick, cursing himself for being so stupid. With him off the ice, the Avalanche quickly capitalized, forcing the play into the Eagles' end and shooting rocket after rocket at Alfonse. Finally, a rebound was poked in, and the score was 1–0, Avalanche.

For the next period and a half, it remained that way. Derek kept his temper, even though Chevy kept up the trash talk, joined now by Regan, who had evidently decided he could get away with it.

Then, at the start of the third period, disaster struck. It started when the puck rolled on its edge into the Avalanche end. Derek, the nearest Eagle, chased after it. Regan and Chevy converged on him from either side. They wound up slamming into Derek like a pair of bricks.

He went down, then got up angry. He shoved Regan to the ice, then turned to Chevy, taking off his gloves and showing his bare fists.

The ref's whistle blew immediately. Chevy backed away, letting the ref and others restrain Derek. Again, that mocking grin was on Chevy's face.

Chris wanted more than anything to wipe it off for him. But he would be on the bench now, with the penalty killing unit on the ice again.

It added insult to injury when Chevy scored the

next goal. He skated around in triumph, being sure to pass right by the penalty box, just in case Derek wanted to spend even more time in there.

Derek emerged fuming, but focused. He looked at Chris and nodded slowly. Chris understood. Derek wanted the puck.

As usual, Derek took the face-off. This time, he made sure it went to Chris. Chris skated in, going around Regan so fast that the larger boy wound up falling to the ice. Chris drew the goalie out toward him as he skated in. The defense collapsed toward the center to stop him.

Now! Chris fed the puck to his right, where Derek was following right behind the defensemen. Derek took the puck and flipped it into the upper corner of the net. Score, Eagles! They had cut the deficit in half, and Chris could feel the momentum swinging their way.

"Stay on, line one!" Coach Berman called out. Derek went to the face-off circle. Now it was he who was wearing the mocking grin, and Chevy and Regan who were steaming.

Chris saw them whispering to each other, then

staring at Derek with hatred in their eyes. A chill went up Chris's spine. What were they planning now?

On the next rush, there was a mad scramble for the puck in the Avalanche end. Chevy came flying at Derek from behind, then deliberately fell to the ground just behind him and rolled into the back of Derek's legs. Derek started to fall, but just then, Regan happened to stumble forward, falling on top of Derek as his legs collapsed under Chevy's weight. There was a horrible snapping sound, and Derek screamed in agony.

A sudden hush came over the crowd. Chevy and Regan struggled to free themselves from the fallen Derek. "Get off him!" the referee shouted. Coach Berman ran out onto the ice along with the opposing coach.

"Is there a doctor in the house?" the ref called out, and two women in the bleachers got up and were helped over to Derek's side. Derek was moaning, but Chris couldn't see through the crowd surrounding him.

"Get a stretcher — this leg is badly broken!" one of the doctors ordered.

"Hurry!" yelled the other.

Chris watched it all happen as if he were dreaming. It was his nightmare coming true. Derek was carried off on a stretcher, his leg bent at a weird angle below the knee. He was thrashing in pain, biting down on a towel, tears flowing from his tightly shut eyes. Ambulance sirens sounded outside the arena.

Before play resumed, Coach Berman huddled with the Eagles. "All right, we've got to suck it up and rise to the moment," he told his team. "It looks like we're gonna be without Derek, and not just for tonight. Broken legs don't heal in a week. For now, let's move Jason Chernick up to right wing on line one. We'll play longer shifts on defense. Right now, we need to score a goal. Let's win this one for Derek!"

The Eagles all cheered at the top of their lungs, and they played their hearts out, too. But Chris's line had lost its rhythm. Jason was much slower than Derek, and Chris and Ricky couldn't adjust. They did not score that period, nor did any of the other lines.

With one minute left to go, Coach Berman pulled Alfonse for an extra winger — and the Avalanche scored an empty-net goal. Final score, 3–1.

The Eagles had lost their first game of the season. They'd lost their undefeated status to a team that played dirty. Worst of all, they'd lost their hero, their star, their leader, their MVP.

Could they really beat this same team next week without Derek?

And what about Derek? How badly was he hurt? Would he ever be able to play hockey again?

The next day, Chris went to see his friend. They'd brought him home from the hospital, but Derek was in a cast, sitting in a big chair with a pair of metal crutches by his side.

"Man," Chris said, shaking his head and looking at his friend. "I can't believe this."

"What I can't believe," Derek said, "is that you all didn't go out and win that game, yo!"

"Sorry. It wasn't like we weren't trying. It just . . . it kind of kicked the stuffing out of us, y'know?"

"Man." Derek shook his head disgustedly.

"Does it hurt bad?" Chris asked.

"You really want to know, I could break your leg for you."

"No thanks," Chris said with a grin. "How long do you have to wear that thing?"

"Six weeks, then three months of therapy. I've got a couple pins in there now."

"Pins!"

"Yeah, to hold the bone together."

"So, what did they say about playing hockey?"

Derek looked down at his cast glumly, and shrugged. "I dunno. Maybe next season . . . maybe never. . . ."

"Is that what they said?" Chris gasped, stunned.

"They said it depends how it heals, and how hard I work on it."

"Well, then, I mean, you're gonna work hard, right?"

Derek stared at the cast. "I dunno. Maybe it's just a white man's game. . . ."

"Shut up!" Chris shouted at him, suddenly angry. "You can't let kids like that run the world. You've got to fight back! Derek, if you don't come back next year and play, they'll have won!"

"They'll have won if you let them beat you next week," Derek said. "Chris, you gotta promise to kick their booties."

Chris smiled. "I'd like to promise," he said, "but

how are we going to beat them without you? I mean, you scored half our goals!"

Derek's trademark scowl came over his face. He leaned over toward Chris and grabbed his shirt with both hands. "*You've* gotta do it," he said in a hoarse whisper. "You the man, little guy. You've got the speed and the moves. You're gonna have to take the shots."

"But what about Ricky?" Chris said.

"Ricky ain't got no shot!" Derek said dismissively. "Make him set screens for you, give you feeds and stuff. But you've gotta shoot — and you'd better put it in, you hear?"

Chris gently removed Derek's hands from his shirt. "I don't know," he said doubtfully. "My shot's not that hard. Nothing like yours, anyway."

"I'll work with you," Derek promised. "Between now and then. Teach you how to get more wrist into the shot."

"Derek, you're on crutches."

"Doesn't matter," Derek insisted. "You get some kids down to the rink on off nights, when the team isn't practicing. You pick me up and drop me off. I'll do the rest."

Chris let a slow grin come over his face. If nothing else, it would get Derek out of his glum mood, get him moving around, get him motivated to work on his recovery. "Sounds like a plan," Chris said.

"Ayiight! We're gonna win. You'll see, dog. I'm telling you now, so you heard it here first."

"Oh, by the way," Chris said, suddenly remembering. "Coach said he's going to bring someone up from Town League to replace you."

"Play on the line with you?"

"No, defense. Chernick's taking your spot on the line."

"Defense, huh?" Derek said, thinking.

"I was thinking about my friend. You know, Lynne?"

"Huh? A girl? Man, you crazy? Wanna bring a girl up to Traveling League for the championship game?"

"She's tough, Derek. You'll see. I'm gonna get her to practice with us. She decked me once. My butt still remembers how that felt."

"Ayiight. You bring her. But man, forget that stuff. No girl is ever gonna play in my place!"

" 'Scuse me for saying so, but isn't that kind of like saying 'No black kids play hockey'?"

Derek scowled at him darkly. "Say what?"

"Well, isn't it the same kind of thing?"

Derek grew thoughtful. "I guess so, now that you mention it," he admitted, backing down. "You're kinda different, ain'tcha, little guy?"

"Different?"

"You see things different. Guess that's why you're okay." He shook Chris's hand affectionately. "Okay, you're gonna win me that game, right? Now go on, get out of here before I beat the stuffing out of you for your big mouth!"

Chris laughed as he left the room, and he could hear Derek's hearty laughter behind him. Well, he guessed he'd cheered his friend up, all right. But how would Derek be feeling if Chris and the Screaming Eagles failed to win the game next weekend?

Chris got Lynne to come down to the rink easily enough. All he had to do was mention the fact that Jason Chernick would be there.

"But take my advice," Chris had warned her. "If you want him to like you, don't act all girly and moony. That's why he always ignores you after the games."

"He does ignore me," Lynne said, pouting. "He acts like I don't exist."

"You want to exist in his world? Just play good hockey. That's all he cares about. Play good, and take my word for it, he'll notice you."

Chris managed to get Alfonse Ferrugia to stand in goal, and Ricky LaSalle had shown up as well. To help Lynne on defense, Chris had brought in Felix Mendez, Jason's old linemate.

Derek sat on the team's bench, shouting out instructions to Chris. "Not like that, fool! You've got to keep the backswing under control. Then lead down with your hip. That's it! You see what kind of leverage you got?"

By the end of the practice session, Chris's shot had definitely improved. But the real revelation of the day had been Lynne St. James.

"So who's the babe?" Jason asked Chris as they took off their skates in the boys' locker room. "Is she your girlfriend or something?"

Chris nearly lost his cookies. "You mean Lynne?"

"Like, duh, she was the only girl there. Who else do you think I mean?"

"No! She's not my girlfriend. We're next-door neighbors. She's like my sister or something. I mean, we've known each other since kindergarten!"

Chris could feel himself blushing. Luckily, Jason wasn't looking at him. He was staring into space, with a little smile on his face.

"Not your girlfriend, huh?" Jason nodded, satisfied. "She's a real player, man. I mean, she can really hit!"

"I know," Chris agreed. "She decked me once so hard I saw stars!"

"Awesome!" Jason grinned. "You know what? She should play for us next weekend!"

Chris felt a thrill go through him. "You really think so?"

"Why not, man? The other team will be afraid to hit her. I mean, who wants to hit a girl, right? We sure didn't just now, and that's when she hits them — *bam!* Down they go. I love it!"

"You think Coach will go for it?"

"If we all tell him to, and she comes to practice

tomorrow night, he'll give her a shot, right? Hey, what have we got to lose?"

"Can't hurt to try," Chris agreed.

Feeling optimistic, and proud of himself for helping Lynne, he went out into the lobby where she was waiting for them. Giving a little nod toward Jason, Chris gave her the thumbs-up sign. She beamed, her face reddening, and nodded excitedly, her eyes sparkling with pleasure.

"Come to practice tomorrow night," Jason told her. "We might have a surprise for you."

At Wednesday night's practice, Chris showed up with Lynne in tow. They walked into the arena together, helping Derek between them. He had an arm thrown over each of their shoulders. Jason Chernick came in behind them, carrying Derek's crutches along with his own gear.

A loud cheer went up from the Eagles when they saw Derek. They all skated over to slap him five and pat him on the back. "You playing Saturday?" Alfonse asked jokingly.

"Don't tempt me, man," Derek shot back, flashing a grin. "Listen up, Coach, I got us a sub."

Coach Berman had come over to greet Derek along with his players. "Oh yeah?" Coach asked. "He'd better be good to fill your shoes."

"There's nobody gonna fill my shoes," Derek said. "I've got big feet. But this girl's good."

It was like Derek had dropped a bomb. A moment of total silence was followed by a loud eruption of laughter. "A girl!" Coach roared. "That's good — oh, that's rich."

"I'm not foolin' with you," Derek said. "Lynne, yo, show 'em what you got."

Lynne stepped forward, in full uniform. "Hi, everyone," she greeted them all. They stared back at her dumbly, not knowing how to react.

"You're not serious," Coach Berman said in a low, worried voice.

"I am," Derek insisted. "Yo, Jason, tell 'em."

"She's good, Coach," Jason confirmed. "She's quick, and she's tough as nails on D."

"She knocked me out cold once," Chris put in, unafraid now to admit it.

Alfonse spoke up. "Coach," he said, then simply nodded.

Coach Berman cleared his throat. "Look, uh . . . there's . . . there's never been a girl in Traveling League . . . and, uh, this is a big game — the biggest. I can't risk —"

134

"You're allowed to appoint a sub for me, right?" Derek asked.

"Well, yeah, but —"

"Try her out, Coach," Jason suggested.

Coach cleared his throat again. "Oh, all right. Just for tonight. I guess we have nothing to lose, giving her a tryout. We wanna be fair, of course. No sex discrimination. But you understand, this is an all-star team?" he asked Lynne.

She nodded excitedly, eager to get the chance to prove herself. And over the next two hours, she did. Several times, she stopped odd-man rushes all by herself, not letting Chris or anyone else get a good shot off at Alfonse. Twice she decked players, although Chris noticed she seemed to take it easier on Jason Chernick.

Chris stole a glance or two at Coach and saw that he was gazing at Lynne, wide-eyed. When it was almost nine o'clock, he said, "Okay, you all go and get changed, then gather on the bench here. I want to talk to you all after I've made a phone call."

He turned to Lynne. "That goes for you, too," he said, looking very serious. Then he went off to make his call.

"Do you think he's gonna let her be on the team?" Chris asked Jason as they changed.

"I don't know, but she's mad tough out there! Did you see her knock Ricky down? She wasn't even going for him. I mean, she just brushed against him, and down he went. Man!" Jason grinned and shook his head admiringly. Chris got a faint whiff of a notion that maybe he liked Lynne back.

Out on the team bench again, Coach came right to the point. "I've just called the commissioner," he announced. "He agrees with me that I have the authority to add an emergency team member of my choice for Saturday's game. Now, I really ought to go back to my original tryout list and see who I cut last. But I liked the way this young lady played tonight." He gave Lynne a nod, and Chris saw her rise in her seat, giddy with the compliment.

"I know there's never been a girl in Traveling League. But I also understand Derek was the league's first-ever African-American player. Sooner or later, barriers have to be broken. And if we don't break them down when we get a gift-wrapped opportunity like this, when are we ever going to?"

He turned to Lynne again. "Lynne St. James, wel-come to the team. Everybody give a shout out for the newest Screaming Eagle!"

The cheer rocked the walls of the arena. The same bunch of guys who, not two hours ago, had nearly choked on the thought of a girl playing on their team, were now all for it. Chris grinned from ear to ear, wondering what they would say if they knew that Lynne had turned twelve years old only a week ago!

The big day had come, and the Screaming Eagles, along with parents, fans, and Derek Morgan — their honorary assistant coach — boarded the buses for the trip to Stone Creek.

The arena there was full of screaming Avalanche supporters. It was the largest, noisiest crowd Chris had seen yet.

Derek took his place on the team bench, beside Chris and Lynne. "Y'all gotta come out smokin'," he reminded the two of them, in case they'd forgotten. He'd only told them thirteen thousand times on the way. Derek seemed hyper, like he wanted to jump out of his cast and skate to center ice. But all he could do was watch as Jason Chernick took the opening face-off — and lost it.

The kid named Chevy led the Avalanche rush into the Eagles' zone. Chris watched from down-ice as Lynne skated over to stop him. Chevy held the puck in the corner behind the net, but Lynne was all over him, forcing him to give it up or freeze it. He froze it, then shot a stunned glance at her.

"Hey!" he cried, pointing. "It's a girl! They've got a girl playing for them!"

Suddenly, the whole arena was buzzing. Lynne had deliberately come in wearing her hair in a pony-tail tucked into the back of her jersey. No one had noticed, until now.

The Avalanche bench was pointing at her now, whispering and laughing. Only Chevy wasn't laughing. He was obviously annoyed that a girl had forced him to freeze the puck.

Jason lost the face-off again, with Regan taking it and passing to Chevy at the point. Again Lynne charged him, startling him so that the puck dribbled off his stick. As he went for it, so did she, smashing into him from the side and knocking him to the ice!

"Hey, ref! Where's the penalty?" Chevy complained.

"Clean hit," the ref said. "She was going for the puck, not the body."

Chevy shot Lynne a murderous look, but she paid no attention. Chris skated over to her and said, "Watch it — that kid's the one who messed up Derek's leg. And he did it on purpose."

"I'm a girl," Lynne reminded him. "He's not going to break my leg. I might break his, though, if he tries." She grinned, and Chris smiled back.

"I told them you were tough," he said. "Hang in there. You're doing great!"

Jason finally won a face-off and flicked the puck back to Lynne. Wasting not an instant, she fired it off the boards, right onto Chris's stick as he flew into the Avalanche zone. The defensemen were caught flat-footed, and Chris zoned in on the goalie alone.

He wound up, the roar of the crowd in his ears. Then he led with his hips, just the way Derek had showed him, and fired the puck down low, the way Coach had told him. The goalie hit the ice, but it was too late. Chris's rocket shot had found its mark.

The Eagles' bench erupted, with Derek pounding his crutches on the Plexiglas. "Yeah, man! That's my dog! Ayiight!"

Chris skated over and high-fived them all. "Now that was a shot!" Derek told him.

"Just getting started," Chris replied as he took a seat on the bench, awaiting his next turn on the ice.

The Avalanche did not play dead for long. Realizing that, without Derek, the Eagles were short on offense, they brought their defensemen up, almost to the Eagles' blue line. This put intense pressure on the Eagles' defense, which didn't have Jason Chernick to lead the way.

Time after time, Chevy, Regan, and the other Avalanche forwards got wicked shots off. But Alfonse was having his best game of the season, fending them off one after another. Several shots were blocked by Lynne St. James, who kept dropping to the ice, putting her body in the way of the puck. After one period, the score was still 1–0, Eagles.

"Gotta get on top again," Derek muttered in Chris's ear. "They've got their defense way up. You can sneak behind it. If somebody gets the puck out to you, you've got another breakaway."

"Got it," Chris said, nodding intently. He knew it was up to him to score. The Avalanche defense was big and tough, and could pretty much stop all the other Eagles from getting into their zone. Their redline trap kept gumming up the passing lanes, making an impenetrable barrier. Only Chris had the speed to break through it. If he didn't score, sooner or later the Avalanche would.

For the first half of the second period, the play was centered in the Eagles' zone. The Avalanche, particularly Regan and Chevy, were coming hard at Lynne, banging into her to try and soften her up. But Lynne wasn't buckling. She was taking their best shots and giving back a few of her own. Twice more, Chevy wound up flat on his back, and Regan wound up getting flattened into the boards so hard that he had to sit out for several minutes.

Finally, with just a few minutes left in the period, Lynne grabbed a misfired pass from an Avalanche forward and sent it through the gap in the defense. Chris grabbed it at the red line, where he'd been waiting, playing possum. He got his feet going in a hurry, then slipped the puck through the legs of the one remaining defenseman, doing a spin at the same time to get around him and retrieve the puck on the other side.

The crowd gasped at the sheer audacity of the move, and the incredible grace and skill with which Chris had pulled it off. But the best was yet to come. Chris faked a slap shot, then flicked it over the goalie as he sank to his knees, biting on the fake. Score!

Now it was 2–0, Eagles, and the Avalanche were starting to panic. Chris watched them as they huddled, taking a time-out. He grinned to Derek, flashing the thumbs-up sign. Derek thumped himself on the chest and pointed at Chris, showing his appreciation.

The time-out must have done the Avalanche some good, because they came out all fired up. They proceeded to bombard Alfonse with shots until they finally scored a goal, just before the period ended. ·

The third period started with the game still very much up for grabs. "They'll be looking to shut you down now," Derek warned Chris. "You'd better concentrate on dishin' off, or dumping the puck into their zone." Turning to Lynne, he added, "You're doin' all right, yo. Come on, now — don't let up. This is payback time, ayiight?"

"I hear that," Lynne agreed, smiling and touching fists with Derek. "Watch me now."

The Eagles fended off the frenzied Avalanche attack for the next ten minutes of play, but then Regan tied the score on a power play, with Jason Chernick in the penalty box.

While Jason was in the box, Chris heard Coach Berman tell him, "If we get the lead again, I'm putting you back on defense."

Jason nodded, and Chris made it his personal business to get that lead back.

"Let me take the next face-off," he told Jason and Ricky.

"You haven't taken one all year," Jason pointed out.

"Come on, let me try once," Chris insisted.

"Oh, okay. I'll back you up. Go ahead."

Chris took the face-off and won it. Not only that, he managed somehow to retain control of the puck and skate on in along the boards, chased by both Chevy and Regan.

He flicked the puck in front of the goal, just as their heavy bodies crunched into his. Chris crumbled to the ice in agony. He wasn't sure if his ribs were broken, but he was sure he couldn't breathe.

It took him a few minutes to get his wind back and make sure there were no broken bones. But when he got up, he saw that the Avalanche were celebrating. They'd scored while he was down on the ice and taken the lead!

Chris shot a worried look at Derek, who was pounding his fist on the Plexiglas in frustration. Chris sat on the bench waiting for his next turn, determined to get his team back into the lead, even if it killed him.

"Line change!" When Chris heard the coach's order he leaped onto the ice, just as the puck was coming his way. He took it on his stick, and quick-passed it to Jason Chernick. Jason carried the puck into the Avalanche zone and fired a blast from the point that somehow found the net.

"Yeah!" Jason shouted.

"All right!" Chris yelled, fired up now that the game was tied again.

There wasn't much time left now. Chris would be

on the ice for just one or two more shifts. He had to score — he just had to!

Chevy led the Avalanche into the Eagles' zone again, and this time Lynne was on the bench. He fired a shot that got past Alfonse — and hit the post!

"Line change!" Chris leaped back onto the ice, and skated for an open spot. Wikki Withers spotted him and sent the puck caroming off the boards to him. Chris took the puck in full stride, with Jason Chernick right behind him. Chris crashed the defense, leaving the puck behind him for Jason to get off a shot. The goalie stopped it with his stick, but it bounced right out to where Chris was standing.

Thwack! Chris sent it right back at the goalie, who never even saw it. The shot hit the post — and ricocheted into the net just as the final buzzer sounded!

They'd won! Chris looked up at the scoreboard with tears dimming his vision. 4–3, in favor of the visiting Screaming Eagles — the new champions of Traveling League!

As soon as he could get out from under the pile of Screaming Eagles, Chris skated over to the bench and hugged Derek. "I couldn't have done it without you!" he said, gasping for breath. His ribs hurt, but

Chris didn't care. His heart was bursting with happiness.

"Whoo-hoo!" Lynne yelled, skating over and hugging Jason.

Chris laughed and shook his head. Lynne might be a devoted hockey player, but romance was never far from her consciousness.

Jason hugged her back, and Chris could see him noticing her now, as if for the first time. A big smile broke out on Jason's face as he gazed into Lynne's eyes, and Chris saw her knees buckle briefly.

Chris smiled a secret smile as he heard Jason say, "Man, you're fantastic!"

"Thanks," Lynne breathed, staring up at Jason with huge blue eyes.

"Say, umm, um, you wanna go get a soda or something after the game?"

"I guess . . . ," Lynne said, trying to sound casual.

"Yessss!" Chris whispered, pumping his fist.

Noticing him, Lynne blushed beet red, but she was smiling like the Cheshire cat. "Thanks," she mouthed silently, and Chris nodded, knowing what she meant.

"Hey!" Coach Berman said, coming over to clap

Chris on the back and shake his hand. "Guess what, kid? You're the MVP of the game!" He handed Chris a nice-sized trophy. Chris took it, dumbfounded.

"And you," he added, turning to Derek, "are the MVP of the season!" Reaching down, he picked up a huge trophy and handed it to Derek, who took it slowly, carefully, his eyes welling up with tears.

"Yo, thanks," he muttered, fighing the urge to cry. "I 'preciate it."

"Come on, Eagles!" Coach called to the rest of the giddy bunch. "Time for a team picture with the trophies!"

The two friends posed with their team, hoisting their trophies. When it was over, they exchanged statues, admiring each other's trophies.

"You did what I told you," Derek said simply "You came through for me."

"I did it for me, if you really want to know," Chris said. "Well, maybe a little for you, too."

"Come on, team, let's go shake hands with the Avalanche," Coach called.

"You gonna go?" Derek asked Chris warily.

"I guess," Chris said. "No sense in having hard

feelings, right? I mean, we got them back where it counted."

"I guess," Derek said, scowling. "At least I don't have to. This leg of mine's still good for something, huh?"

They shared a laugh, and Chris skated out to shake hands. Chevy muttered a curse as Chris stuck his hand out, but Chris ignored it and shook his hand anyway. Whatever Chevy's problem was, it was his — not Chris's, not Derek's. Chevy would have to deal with it someday. Something told Chris he would only learn the hard way.

"Honey!" Chris's mom greeted him when he finally came off the ice. "I'm so proud of you!"

"Thanks, Mom," Chris told her. "Thanks for letting me play hockey."

"I was wrong about you not being tough enough," she admitted.

"And I was wrong for giving up figure skating," he offered. "No reason I can't do both."

They hugged hard, and Chris was happy because he'd made his mom happy.

It was the best day of his whole life — but Chris had a feeling there were even better days to come!

Matt Christopher®

Muhammad Ali

Lance Armstrong

Kobe Bryant

Jennifer Capriati

Dale Earnhardt, Sr.

Jeff Gordon

Ken Griffey Jr.

Mia Hamm

Tony Hawk

Ichiro

Derek Jeter

Randy Johnson

Michael Jordan

Mario Lemieux

Mark McGwire

Yao Ming

Shaquille O'Neal

Jackie Robinson

Alex Rodriguez

Babe Ruth

Curt Schilling

Sammy Sosa

Venus and Serena
Williams

Tiger Woods

The #1 Sports Series for Kids

Read them all!

- Baseball Flyhawk
- Baseball Pals
- Baseball Turnaround
- The Basket Counts
- Body Check
- Catch That Pass!
- Catcher with a Glass Arm
- Catching Waves
- Center Court Sting
- Centerfield Ballhawk
- Challenge at Second Base
- The Comeback Challenge
- Comeback of the Home Run Kid
- Cool as Ice
- The Diamond Champs
- Dirt Bike Racer
- Dirt Bike Runaway
- Dive Right In
- Double Play at Short
- Face-Off
- Fairway Phenom
- Football Fugitive
- Football Nightmare
- The Fox Steals Home
- Goalkeeper in Charge
- The Great Quarterback Switch
- Halfback Attack*
- The Hockey Machine
- Ice Magic
- Inline Skater
- Johnny Long Legs
- The Kid Who Only Hit Homers

*Previously published as Crackerjack Halfback

Lacrosse Face-Off

Line Drive to Short**

Long-Arm Quarterback

Long Shot for Paul

Look Who's Playing First Base

Miracle at the Plate

Mountain Bike Mania

Nothin' But Net

Penalty Shot

Prime-Time Pitcher

Red-Hot Hightops

The Reluctant Pitcher

Return of the Home Run Kid

Roller Hockey Radicals

Run For It

Shoot for the Hoop

Shortstop from Tokyo

Skateboard Renegade

Skateboard Tough

Slam Dunk

Snowboard Champ

Snowboard Maverick

Snowboard Showdown

Soccer Duel

Soccer Halfback

Soccer Scoop

Stealing Home

The Submarine Pitch

The Team That Couldn't Lose

Tennis Ace

Tight End

Top Wing

Touchdown for Tommy

Tough to Tackle

Wingman on Ice

The Year Mom Won the Pennant

All available in paperback from Little, Brown and Company

**Previously published as Pressure Play